My Nutty Neighbours

'...cups'

THE IRISH TIMES

'Full marks for originality and readability'

BOOKS IRELAND

'Such an enjoyable read –

hilarious one-liners'

CHILDREN'S BOOKS IN IRELAND

WHAT THEY SAID ABOUT **Cherokee**

'Original, beautifully fresh'

ROBERT DUNBAR, CHILDREN'S BOOKS IN IRELAND

'A major find'

BOOKS IRELAND

Creina Mansfield has a Master's degree in novel writing from Manchester University. She likes both dogs and cats, and fosters kittens in her spare time. She has written *My Nasty Neighbours,* a companion to this book; *Cherokee*, a novel about a young boy and his grandfather who both love to play jazz; *Fairchild*; and, for younger readers, *Snip, Snip!* in which a little obsession with scissors leads to interesting situations.

My Nutty Neighbours

Creina Mansfield

THE O'BRIEN PRESS
DUBLIN

First published 2006 by The O'Brien Press Ltd,
20 Victoria Road, Dublin 6, Ireland.
Tel: +353 1 4923333; Fax: +353 1 4922777
E-mail: books@obrien.ie
Website: www.obrien.ie

ISBN-10: 0-86278-788-2
ISBN-13: 978-0-86278-788-2

British Library Cataloguing-in-Publication Data
Mansfield, Creina
My nutty neighbours
1.Parent and teenager - Juvenile fiction 2.Neighbors - Juvenile fiction
3.Country life - Juvenile fiction 4.Children's stories
I.Title
823.9'14[J]

1 2 3 4 5 6 7 8 9 10
06 07 08 09 10 11 12

The O'Brien Press
receives assistance from

Editing, typesetting, layout and design: The O'Brien Press Ltd
Cover illustration: Kate Sheppard
Printing: Cox & Wyman Ltd

DEDICATION

To Rob, once Bob, with as much love as ever.

ACKNOWLEDGEMENTS

Thanks to the team at The O'Brien Press,
particularly my editor, Rachel Pierce.

Contents

Unready!

'**D**avid! If you're not ready and down here in five minutes, I'm leaving without you! David? *David!*' There was a crash and a yell, followed by the sort of language that gets me a detention at school; aren't parents meant to set a good example? Dad had obviously tripped over my dog.

Ready. Was I *ready* for school? I lay in bed thinking about this, as curses and growls floated up the winding staircase to my attic room. Overall, taking all aspects of the situation into account and looking at it objectively, I think I would have to say – not. Definitely not ready. Or was there such a word as *unready*? If there was, I had a lot of use for it. I was unready for Maths, my first class, as I hadn't done the homework. Ditto French in third period and History in fifth. Unready for the long, boring ride into the centre of Dublin with Dad. Most of all I was unready for what would happen at rugby practice, when classes were over …

Now lunch, on the other hand, lunch I would be ready for, having missed out on breakfast. *Breakfast!* I had finally found a reason to get out of bed. I was dressed in two minutes, had my bag packed in three and with my tie in my teeth I vaulted over the banisters and was in the kitchen with seconds still on the clock!

Dad was at the kitchen table, suited and booted, his briefcase at his side, jangling his keys impatiently. He made a point of massaging his knee when he saw me.

'Oh, so you've condescended to appear, have you?' he said sourly. 'I wish you'd exercise that dog of yours in the morning. You promised you would when you asked … *begged* us to buy it for you. Then perhaps he wouldn't skulk at the bottom of the stairs. I nearly broke my neck!'

'He didn't get hurt, did he?' I asked quickly.

'Oh no, he's just fine,' said Dad bitterly. 'Get your priorities right, why don't you?'

And there we had it, the first parental anomaly of the day. It was a disturbingly frequent occurrence in our house, the parental anomaly: a clear direction followed by an immediate contradiction. He had just told me my dog was meant to be my priority! Knowing it would take too much effort to get this point across to him, I just said, between gulpfuls of Coco Pops, 'I'll walk him when I get home.'

'Get a move on. We're already late. I've told you before, if we leave any later than 7.45, we get snarled up in traffic on the Long Mile Road.'

'Your choice to live out here!' I said cheerfully. Cheerfully because I knew it would wind him up. Mum and Dad were always giving me the lecture about the choices you make having consequences. *With freedom comes responsibility*, blah blah blah. Well, they were responsible for us moving out of Dublin and into the back of beyond. Our address is:

> The Stirling family
> *The Haven*
> Ballykreig
> County Kildare
> Ireland.

I'm still trying to figure out why Mum and Dad renamed the old house *The Haven* – *Stirlings' Folly* would be closer to the truth. Or *Windy Way* might hint at how tiny air currents became swirling tempests by the time they'd reached the top of the hill on which, two hundred years ago, some idiot decided to build the place. Most days there were so many draughts it was like living in a wind tunnel.

Okay, the house *is* impressive. It's the biggest in the area, standing in what the slick fella who sold us the place called '*its own substantial grounds*', which roughly translates as there's enough grass to keep me mowing all weekend. And of course it's *my* job because I'm the strongest, although my brother Ian makes out it's because I'm younger than him and my sister, Helen. The truth is he's such a wimp he doesn't have the strength to pull the starter cord on the lawn mower! And Helen might break a nail, which would, of course, be a tragedy.

Inside, the house is impressive too. Lots of 'features' – such as a huge kitchen, brand new but made to look as if it's out of an old farmhouse. It cost Mum and Dad thousands. Make sense to you? No, it doesn't to me either.

We used to live in civilisation with shops, cinemas and luxuries like pavements. I used to walk to school. Now, St Joseph's is a time zone away.

'*The Haven's splendid and charming – a real find,*' Mum tells her friends, as if she's swallowed the estate agent's dictionary. She tells them on the phone, though, because we're too far out for them to visit. With their less-than-razor-sharp minds, Mum and Dad had forgotten to take into consideration that if we lived miles *from* anywhere, then it was miles *to* anywhere. At *The Haven*, a busy day is when a pheasant strolls by. Why, oh why did my life have to go so horribly wrong?

It was no stroll driving into Dublin with Dad. He pounded the roads, lurching around the bends so it was difficult for me to do my homework. My maths ended up looking like this:

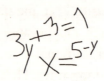

I didn't bother with the French homework. I've got no plans to visit that particular part of the world and if you ask me, the people in the countryside around *The Haven* have enough trouble with English – no way am I going to start spouting French at them! History was another matter, however. Sullivan taught my class History. Nobody messes with Sullivan.

As Dad had 'predicted' (like he was Mystic Meg!), we ground to a dead stop on the Long Mile Road. More cursing and fuming. At least he wanted to get to where he was headed: to work at the Data Protection Offices. Me, I wasn't so keen to get to my destination. The thought of rugby practice at four o'clock hung like a black cloud over the day, which is ironic because I'm seriously good at rugby and am personally, single-handedly responsible for us winning the Cup last season. At St Joseph's the three Rs aren't Reading, 'Riting and 'Rithmetic, but Rugby, Rugby and Rugby. I'd won my place on the A team. I should be riding high, but thanks to my sister, things hadn't quite worked out as I had planned.

Registration was over by the time I sprinted into school. My friends, Joe and Abbas, had covered for me. They were used to me being late. I looked over Abbas' shoulder through Maths and we bombarded the young French assistant with questions so he forgot to ask for our homework (*quelle horreur!*). Things were going well until after lunch break and it was time for History.

We knew Sullivan was in a bad mood from the subtle tell-tale signs, such as the way he grabbed us in pairs by the scruff of our necks and threw us into the classroom. Then he talked in his dull, monotonous voice so that most of the class dozed off with their eyes open. I was one of them, but was jolted awake by Sullivan's shadow falling across my desk.

'So, Stirling, what can we adduce from this?'

This what? Homework had been about the French Revolution, but we might have moved through centuries since then – the class had sure felt like a few hundred years. We could have been up to the Second World War for all I knew. Anyway, from the ugly smile on Sullivan's mug, I could tell he was out to get me, whatever I said.

That only tossers use words like adduce? was the answer he deserved, but seventeen stone of taut, angry muscle was looming in front of me, so I settled for, 'Eh?' This seemed to please him; he beamed around at my classmates. Some of them actually woke up – they sensed trouble as Sullivan sarcastically repeated, '*Eh, eh, eh*', making me sound like a moron. He thumped on my desk, waking the rest of the class before he went on.

'What an intelligent reaction! What I was asking you, *Stirling*, to put it in words of one syllable, was can you give examples of violence being counterproductive?'

I knew he didn't actually expect an answer. He just wanted to sit intimidatingly on the side of my desk and smirk, which he did for a couple of minutes before raising his sizable backside and going back to boring us all senseless talking about *The Terror*. But not before giving me a page to write on '*Why I must concentrate at all times*'.

I made sure he was well out of the way before I turned around and whispered to Abbas, '*Counterproductive* has five syllables!'

What really gets me is that I've got troubles because I'm meant to be Sullivan's *favourite*. None of the rest of the A team is in my History class. If they were, they'd see how the idea that he picks me out for special treatment is crazy. Specially *bad* treatment, yes. Having to sit through his History lessons is pain enough for anyone, but he'll always have a go at me if he gets the chance. St Joseph's sure didn't give him the History job because of his teaching skills. No, Sullivan was on the staff because of his international caps for Ireland. Sullivan was the rugby coach – and my sister's boyfriend.

That day in June should have been the best of my life. The St Joseph's rugby team was in the Cup final. In the last few minutes, with us one point behind, I took a drop-kick and scored! We won and the rest of the team hoisted me on their shoulders to march victoriously around the ground. If I had only known that, at that very moment, my sister Helen was batting her eyelashes at Sullivan. That would have wiped the smile from my mud-smeared face. Before anyone had got around to saying, 'Well done, David. Congratulations for that brilliant kick,' Helen and Sullivan were going out together. They'd become *an item*, as Abbas put it. Some of the boys at school weren't so polite and I'd been in two major fights about it already. Sullivan wore a nauseating grin whenever he looked at my sister, Helen went back to preening herself and Mum and Dad were laughing because for once she had a boyfriend who wasn't older than them. No one bothered to consider what it would be like for *me* having my sister go out with my rugby coach and teacher. It was really unfair because before this 'boyfriend' lark, I got on with Sullivan. I mean, he has played for Ireland – that's something I'd like to do. But now everything was awkward, and on top of that I felt like I was starring in my own personal bad horror movie: no one could see how he was treating me, except me! No matter how well I played, I got snide remarks about how my place on the A team was because of Helen.

'How's your brother-in-law, Stirling?' 'Having the lovely Sullivan round for tea, Stirling?' 'You and Sullivan discussing your rugby career over there, Stirling?'

I was really sick of it, but then, that's pretty much all sisters are good for: ruining your life.

More trouble and
the long trek home

By four o'clock it was raining. The whole squad got into their kit slowly, loitering in the changing rooms, but when Sullivan appeared, it was me he yelled at.

'Not started yet, Stirling?' he barked. 'Come on, lad, round that pitch! You're a wing, not a wuss!'

Frazier jogged by my side, repeating, '*Come on, lad, come on, lad*' in a girly voice, as if Sullivan had said it to be friendly. My elbow accidentally-on-purpose jerked back in Frazier's face, then we were racing around the pitch, with him trying to catch me. I'm a winger – I'm meant to be fast, and I am. No way was Frazier going to get hold of me. I left him standing. Panting, he shouted out between gasps of breath, 'You can run, Stirling, but you can't hide!' I knew he was right. During practice, they would be plenty of opportunities for him to have a go …

Sure enough, when we practiced passing, he positioned himself so he should have thrown to me, but left me out. I let it go once, then twice, but when he did it the third time I rushed forward and intercepted the ball. Let's see how he likes that! I threw the ball on, then stood in front of him and caught the ball when it came his way. Round and round the ball went and each time I intercepted. Finally he'd had enough and he threw himself at my legs, knocking me to the ground. He landed one blow on my ear before I hurled him off with a kick to the stomach. He lay winded, giving me a chance to grab him.

Suddenly, someone was hauling me up by the shoulders. 'What the hell do you think you're doing?' Sullivan shook me round. 'This is team practice, Stirling. Get it? *Team* practice. You're meant to be working together, not against each other.'

He looked down at Frazier, 'You all right, lad?' Frazier stayed on the ground, rubbing his stomach. It was Oscar-winning stuff. He nodded, as if he were being heroically uncomplaining. Only when Sullivan had marched away did he leap up and give me a malevolent grin.

I trudged home in the drizzle after rugby practice, having caught the bus. Though Dad usually took me into Dublin, I often had to make my way back home by glorious public transport because he 'could never be sure what time he would be leaving the office'. I suppose a data protection emergency could arise at any moment! I imagined Dad dressed like a firefighter – though I knew he wore a suit to work – valiantly tackling a mound of data that was heaving down the road, like a mudslide. Whatever he was really doing, it meant I had to sit on the bus for hours. I was too tired to do my 'Why I must concentrate at all times' page of nonsense. I hadn't even had a shower because I'd guessed that Frazier, now with a black eye, planned to ambush me in the changing rooms.

As I looked out the window, watching Dublin giving way to Culchieville, I got to thinking how there's nowhere to walk in the country. I know it looks as if there is, with loads of fields and stuff, but there are no sensible pavements by the side of the roads. Have you ever tried walking through a field of maize? I have, to take a short cut to our house last September, just after we'd moved in. Though I'm tall for my age, I couldn't see over it, got lost and ended up coming out the same side of the field that I'd entered, with scratches on my face and arms. I would sooner fight my way through the front line of St Mary's rugby team. Having got off the bus, I walked along the side of the road, with no pavement and with cars hurtling around the bends, clipping my heels as I dragged my kit through the puddles.

Then she appeared. I'd seen her before a couple of times. She was about my age, with loads of red hair. Very fit. Dead pretty. She was walking the other way from me, as she had been when I'd seen her last time. Before, she'd been wearing a school uniform, but this time she was in jeans and a parka jacket. And she was carrying a couple of golf clubs. We sort of looked at each other as we came around the bend. I tried a nod and a bit of a smile. Casual, so if she didn't want to smile back it was no big deal. Trouble is, I reckon it came out as one of those nods culchies give. A nod they give to everyone because the countryside is so thinly inhabited and they're thrilled to see another human being. A nod that's halfway between a twitch and a wink. A nod that says, *I am simple-minded!*

At the thought of what I must look like, my smile turned to a scowl. Then, a yellow Volkswagen swept past me. I recognised Helen's car and started to wave, thinking she'd stop and give me a lift. I was that wet, cold and hungry, I was prepared to risk my life in her passenger seat. But to see me she would have had to use her rear-view mirror and Helen – who spends hours staring at herself in a mirror, *'Does my bum look big in this?'* – has never used her car's rear-view mirror for its actual purpose. She has it permanently slewed so she can check her make-up. She refuses to hold the steering wheel properly in case she breaks a nail! How she passed her test, I'll never work out. She probably batted her eyelashes and swung her long blonde hair about, like they do in the adverts, and the examiner fell for it. Helen is nineteen but there are kids of nine who'd be safer behind the wheel of a car.

The Queen of Mirrors sped by and I was left looking like a complete idiot dancing up and down in the road. I turned to see if the girl was in sight, but she'd gone. Wait till I see my sister next! She's responsible for my biggest problem. I've compiled a list:

Problems to be solved

1. My sister's going out with my rugby coach, so now I'm meant to be his favourite, which everyone slags me for

endlessly, but in actual fact he treats me even worse than before he hooked up with Helen. *Some favourite!* The man's a slave-driver. So problem one: how do I get him off my back?

2. I live so far out of Dublin, it's a wonder it's on the map. On those old medieval maps, where I live now there'd be blank parchment and a sign: **Here be Dragons**. So how was I meant to see my friends and keep up with everything that's going on? Time spent travelling means less rest time, less telly time and less eating time – all bad. Somehow, I had to convince Mum and Dad to move back to Dublin.

Now I'd got something to add to the list:

3. I'd made myself look stupid in front of the only decent-looking girl within tractor distance, so how was I going to approach her now?

In fact, this latest problem broke down into a whole subset of related problems:

(i) How was I going to find out her name?
(ii) How would I get talking to her, and when I did manage that, what the hell would I say?
(iii) How would I banish the eejit impression and make her see that I was in fact an extremely attractive, hugely interesting, incredibly talented and very cool person?

The toff and the cockney

There was no one in the kitchen, just the usual array of cakes. That was the only good thing about our move from Dublin: Mum had so much time, she cooked everyday. I usually had a choice of five or six different cakes. I could see meringues, chocolatey caramel stuff, a big cake with icing on top and Mum's famous flapjacks. I threw down my wet things and had just started on a second meringue when I heard deep growling sounds. Nope, not my stomach — it was coming from upstairs. I stuffed another cake in my mouth: if that noise was what I thought it was, it could be a while before I got my proper tea.

'Mum!'

I could hear her voice, sweet and cajoling, then nervous and hesitant.

'David, in here!'

I followed her voice and found her in Helen's bedroom on the first floor. Mum and I were silent as the growling continued. It went on so long, it began to sound like a purr. It meant only one thing! So, if you think you have more limbs than you need, you might be tempted to reach forward and pat the smallest, sweetest, cutest, most diabolical dog ever put on this planet. My last birthday present: a black-and-white, long-haired pedigree dog, no bigger than a cat, with round, dark eyes and huge ears, like a butterfly's wings.

'What now?' Hearing my voice, he started to wag his tail, but stopped abruptly.

'He's got one of Helen's hairbrushes caught in his tail. I can't get near him,' Mum explained. The growl deepened and Mum took a few paces back.

'Right. This requires one hundred percent body armour.' I kept my voice even, though I knew he had a sixth sense when we plotted against him. 'Get me a wax jacket and leather gloves.'

Mum rushed away while my dog and I eyeballed each other. I wanted to make sure he didn't slink away to hide under furniture because he could slip into the smallest spaces. When he was guarding a bone, one of us would walk by without seeing him and he'd suddenly shoot out from some hiding place and attack our feet.

Mum came back with my protective clothing. I put it on, making sure there was no gap between jacket and gloves that sharp little teeth could find. They all said this sort of thing was my job because he had been a present to me, but the real reason was that, with my rugby experience, I knew how to face fear head-on. I knew there was no point hesitating. Just go for it.

I threw myself on the dog before he saw me coming. I grabbed the brush and he yelped with pain. The long white hairs of his tail were tangled around it, but I kept on pulling. If I gave up, the second attempt would be more difficult because it would be without the element of surprise. He would go into hiding and it would take an army of vets to get the brush off. I felt it loosen and pulled again, even as he planted his teeth in the sleeve of the wax jacket. I tugged again and the brush finally came free. For a nanosecond he stopped, as if registering that the weight on his tail had gone, then, his eyes fierce, he bit into the jacket in a frenzy of indignation.

I plucked him off. 'You are one crazy dog.' As I put him down, he made a lunge for my feet, but I'd known better than to take off my school boots, so he gave up and retreated behind Helen's dressing table, brooding.

Mum peeked from behind the door. 'Thank goodness! He's been like that for nearly two hours. Oh, David! Look at the mud you've brought in. I've asked you before to change into slippers as soon as you come in.'

'If I'd done that, I'd be missing my toes by now! Hang on … did you say he'd been like that for *two hours*?' I'd seen Helen departing less than half-an-hour earlier. Mum nodded.

'So it happened while Helen was here? Why didn't she do something about it? After all, it's her hairbrush. If she hadn't left it on the floor, he'd never have got it caught. He's too small to climb up onto a dressing table.'

I already knew the answer – Helen avoided anything that might put a speck of dirt on her. Clothes and cosmetics were scattered about her room as if it had been ransacked, but Helen herself always looked immaculate.

'She was rushing to get her hair done,' said Mum, as if that counted as an emergency. Helen should wear one of those panic alarms old people have around their necks. *A speck of dust has landed on my T-shirt* – bleep! *The wind has ruffled my hair* – bleep! *My mascara has run* – bleep! bleep!

Mum started picking up Helen's clothes from the bedroom floor. Helen's untidiness had been one of the reasons Mum and Dad had experimented with us having two houses and living next door to each other, but now Mum was back to being her unpaid servant. 'You okay, Mum?' I noticed she was in her old dressing gown again.

'Me? Oh, I'm fine, love.'

'So why aren't you dressed?'

'Oh, I started cleaning this morning, thought I'd get dressed afterwards, then got into cooking. Nobody's going to call in. It's so quiet here! You know, if Ian wasn't home from college, I wouldn't have seen a soul today.'

'Yeah, I told you being out here's for the living dead. Bet you the countryside is full of daytime pyjama-wearers. Not worth it, if you ask me.' Mum shot me a look. 'Well, I've got the dog to walk.'

The magic word *walk* drew him from his hiding place, his tail wagging. 'Come on.' He drove me mad, but he was cute, loyal and *mine*. Also, he's a pedigree, which is like a toff in the dog world. That's why he doesn't have some doggy name, like Rover. His name is registered with the Kennel Club. It's *Man Of Honour*, though I usually call him M for short.

I got his lead and took him out for a walk, back down the

narrow, winding lanes. I took the same route I'd been using the day before, wondering if maybe I'd see the girl with the red hair again. It was getting dark and cars sped around the bends and swerved away as we came into view. One didn't bother, so we had to jump into the ditch. I was clambering back out when a familiar figure slouched into view.

'Whatcha Bro!'

My brother Ian was carrying a couple of bags. He'd obviously been to the village shop, which was about as much excitement as the neighbourhood offered. All these people with time on their hands and me still with homework to do! We walked back to *The Haven* together, Ian talking and me trying to translate what he said into proper Dublin English. Back from London, where he was studying music, he'd acquired a fake cockney accent. The *Young Musician of the Year* sounded as if he'd been on the set of 'Eastenders'. Last year, he'd abandoned his serious musical ambitions and joined a heavy metal band called *The Oily Rags* – which had been another reason for Mum and Dad opting for dual houses. Ian's drumming had disturbed the neighbours and driven anyone without concrete in their ears entirely mad. Now he was *back on track* as Dad called it, playing piano and violin. Mum and Dad didn't seem to have noticed the fake cockney accent. It was a mockery of a travesty of a farce, if you ask me. Sometimes he sounded so odd I wished for *The Oily Rags* days back again when he'd looked peculiar, but at least sounded close to normal.

By the time we arrived home, M looked like a mop dunked in a bucket of mud. He shook himself clean in the kitchen as we checked out what was for tea.

'Ah, pukka grub,' said Ian.

Mum had made a steak and kidney pie, and a potato and mushroom one for him. He'd become a vegetarian in London, too. Every time he came home to visit he had changed. The only constant was his absorption in music and his weedy body. Flimsy McFeeble. He holds St Joseph's record for avoiding PE. They should have given him a prize for it before he left. He had some good excuses, all the usual ones about his kit being in the wash, or forgetting it, but I particularly like, 'I have a skin condition that means I must avoid mud,' and, 'My violin teacher insists I must rest my right elbow'. Though hopeless at sports and fighting, he was always winning prizes – the McBride piano trophy, the Edward Memorial Scholarship for Outstanding Musical Accomplishment. You get the picture. Being the younger brother of Ian Stirling, he of the angelic voice who won a place at the Royal Academy of Music, sure took some living down. I'd been singing out of tune in Assembly for two years just to prove I wasn't like him.

I get an idea

Why I must concentrate at all times

I must concentrate at all times because it is a good thing to concentrate. If I concentrate, then I will not miss important things that are happening. I dare say some of the most disastrous events in history could have been different if only people had been concentrating. If King Louis of France and Queen Marie Antoinette had been concentrating, they would have noticed that loads of French peasants did not have enough to eat. Then they could have done something about it and they would not have been beheaded by the guillotine. After that event, no way could they concentrate, so then they had a watertight excuse.

If you've got masses to do, it's tough to concentrate all the time. If you live right near the school, then okay, you can get up <u>when it's light</u> and just walk to school. Then you're the one – ooh, look at him, he has ~~phenomnenal~~ exceptional powers of concentration.

No! He's just got an easy life – not even a dog probably, that needs exercising everyday. A sister who gives him lifts in her car. A brother who talks proper English, not some weird

accent so you have to <u>concentrate</u> just to make out what the words are.
David Stirling.

I got to Assembly the next morning by the skin of my teeth, having written my page for Sullivan as Dad and I moved at a snail's pace along the Long Mile Road. I wasn't too happy about the finished product, but it was too late now to change it. Unless I got a chance in French class. Otherwise, Sullivan would expect me to hand it in at the beginning of History class.

The headmaster was making some announcements when a weird thing happened. Maybe it was doing that whole page about concentrating, but suddenly I was actually listening to what he was saying! He was telling us that St Joseph's golf team had lost the match they had played on Saturday. No surprise there. They never won. If there was a category worse than losing, they'd get into it. They were hopeless. But what I noticed was that the headmaster was beaming. If we lost at rugby, he got in a right strop. You'd think we'd done it on purpose to spoil his day. Now he was giving out these rubbish results and *congratulating* the whole golf team for 'putting up a creditable performance'.

'I want some of that,' I whispered to Joe and Abbas. 'Praise for *losing*.' And it got me thinking. There was massive competition for places on the rugby teams, whereas all you had to do to get on the golf team was turn up with some golf clubs. Rugby is a tough, physical game; golf, on the other hand, is only a matter of thwacking a ball. No one is hurtling towards you. No one tackles. I'd never heard of a golf player getting an ear ripped off. Sure, even if it rains, the guys on the telly have a caddy holding an umbrella over them! And the ball they have to hit is stationary. How difficult can that be?

I kept thinking about this during French. With the golf course virtually next door, I could practice whenever I chose. And the girl with the red hair had been carrying golf clubs. If I started going up the range, I'd be bound to see her. I could find out her name and get talking to her. And, after a week or two's practice, she was bound to be impressed by my golf. I could even give her a few tips. I'd have a chance to do that thing that happens in films, where a fella gets up close and personal by showing a girl how to hold a snooker cue, a tennis racket ... or a golf club.

With French class taken up with a fine case of concentrating – okay, not on French – we got to History without me having a chance to rewrite '*Why I must concentrate at all times*'. Luckily, Sullivan took it without a word, flung it onto a pile of scripts and set about boring us senseless, so I was saved – at least for another day.

During lunch break I tried out my idea on Abbas. 'I might take up golf.'

'What?' He dropped a chip. He played rugby too and was on the B team.

'The school golf team could do with some help. You heard what the headmaster said this morning?'

'No.'

'They lost by, like, a million points and he *congratulated* them.'

'Oh, that's what you were on about in Assembly.'

'Well, what do you think?'

'I think you should go back to missing Assembly.'

So, not exactly resounding enthusiasm from my best friend. When Mum and Dad moved us into two houses, we'd lived in Highfield Road, the same street as Abbas and his family. We'd even moved in with them for a while after Mum burned down the houses. Not deliberately. She's not an arsonist. She was just too quick to clear out the grate and the hot cinders set a wooden fireguard alight. Of course, if it had been *me*, you could be sure I'd be visiting a psychiatrist by now and given pages to write on *'Why I must be careful to avoid burning houses to the ground'*.

My friends had come around a lot when I'd been living with Helen and Ian in Highfield Road. It was close to school, we had loads of satellite channels and there were no parents in the house. Perfect! Then, in a careless moment, a so-called responsible adult burned down two entire houses. By then the house Ian, Helen and I were occupying was so dirty that setting a match to it was the quickest way of getting it clean. They still talked about The Great Fire in Highfield Road, so when I went to Abbas' for tea, I made sure I kept my hood up. The Stirlings are Highfield Road's idea of the neighbours from Hell. They make programmes about neighbours like us. Honest, this is what I'm up against.

Even though Abbas wasn't keen, I still liked the golf

idea. It would give me another sport apart from rugby. Sullivan had nothing to do with selecting the golf team, so no one could accuse me of favouritism there. I hadn't said anything about the girl to Abbas, but that was another good reason. I made up my mind to have a go. The first job would be to persuade Dad to buy me some golf clubs.

First nutty neighbour

Helen and Mum were in the kitchen when I got home. I'd seen Helen's yellow Volkswagen parked outside. She was home early from the beauticians where she worked. *Beautiful People* it was called. Give me a break! Bet she spends her days trowelling make-up onto old bags and picking their spots. I tucked into the cakes Mum had put out. Helen groaned. 'How come you can eat so much without getting fat? It's not fair.'

'I exercise. Pile it in, then burn it off,' I explained cheerfully.

'Mum,' whined Helen, 'I wish you didn't bake all the time. It's such a temptation. I want to get down to a size ten before … you know.'

I looked up sharply. Significant glances were being exchanged. Helen was doing the Big Sister this-is-none-of-your-concern routine.

'What?' I asked.

'Don't talk with your mouth full. It's disgusting,' Helen said.

'And picking other people's feet all day isn't?'

'I've told you before, I give pedicures. *Pedicures*. I'm not a chiropodist.'

'Whatever. So ... what's up?'

Helen just looked at her nail polish, but Mum chilled me with her answer. 'We were talking about Helen and Brendan's future.'

'You mean–'

A piece of Battenburg cake went down the wrong way as I realised what she meant. I nearly choked.

'He hasn't proposed yet,' Helen said quickly, 'so don't say anything at school.'

As if! I might just as well send out invitations to stick my head down the toilet.

'You mean they might get ...' I was trying to get out the word *married* when we heard M's frenzied growl coming from the utility room next to the kitchen.

'Not another hairbrush,' sighed Mum.

I ran through, followed by Mum and Helen. M was nipping at something by the washing machine. I grabbed his lead from its hook on the wall. 'M – walk!' I shouted. He turned and it gave me the chance to grab what he had been nipping at. It was a tiny kitten, wide-eyed with fright. I put it on top of the washing machine. It raised a paw, spread its claws and hissed.

'Poor little thing. It's probably feral.' The kitten backed off as Mum went to stroke it.

'What's feral?' I asked.

'Wild. There's probably hundreds around here. Some would be farm cats. None of them neutered. This one's probably been abandoned by its mother.'

'Quick, David, get the poor thing some milk,' said Helen.

'Why don't you get it?'

'Oh, it's so *cuteee* ...' Mum and Helen were obviously smitten.

'It's probably not hungry. It was eating out of M's bowl. No wonder he went for it.' I was glad to have an excuse for his behaviour. 'I wouldn't like it if someone was eating off my plate.' M was restless. 'I'd better take him for a walk.' Mum was offering the kitten a saucer of milk and it was slowly edging towards her.

'Great!' I said to M as we left. 'Now I'm going to be related to my rugby coach. Then absolutely nobody'll believe I got my place fairly!' If I had to jump into a ditch on this walk, I'd be tempted to stay there as the reality of being Sullivan's brother-in-law sank in, so I took a different route, over the fields. It gave me a chance to thrash about with a stick and think. I had to get those golf clubs! Given the way things were going, I definitely needed a Plan B sport. There was every chance that my school rugby career was about to be kicked to touch. I mean, if Sullivan was this sadistic when he was my sister's boyfriend, what was he going to be like when he was her fiancé? Plan B – golf!

But how was I going to get my hands on a decent set of clubs? If I'd wanted a ukulele or a trombone or some such musical instrument, Mum and Dad would be falling over themselves to buy it. They'd spent thousands on violins and pianos for Ian over the years and now Dad said it was costing megabucks to keep him while he studied in London. He hadn't got a vacation job because he said getting into Dublin would take too much time. This is the journey I did six days a week! I'd suggested that Ian visit the neighbouring farms and offer his services, but apparently Flimsy McFeeble couldn't do manual labour because he had to protect his hands. It is the best get-out ever. If M gets a twig entwined in his hair, Ian refuses to help in case M bites his hand. Likewise with helping Dad in the garden. Even mowing the lawn might do irreparable damage to those delicate hands of his. I'm surprised he is prepared to open the door for himself – he could get a bruise off a faulty doorknob.

I came out of the fields onto a winding lane with some small, modern bungalows along it. The first bungalow had a nice garden, but the second was like a little shantytown, like pictures of Mexico City. From the back wall to the house there were buildings made out of bits of wood, corrugated metal and even cardboard. There was just a narrow path down the middle of the sheds. I saw a red bouncing blob moving along the path towards me. A face suddenly turned upwards to stare at me. I'd been watching the top of a red baseball cap.

I was going to give him one of those culchie nod/winks when he beat me to it. Only the gesture I got was a two-fingered one. He muttered something, and then moved away.

So much for the friendliness of simple countryfolk!

Crazy as a coot! Does he think I want to nick some of his junk? With neighbours like that …

By the time M and I got back from our walk, the kitten was sleeping on a blanket in a shoebox. Ian was leaning over to look at it as he lay curled asleep. 'Look at Mozart's whiskers. Ah, in't 'e luverley?'

'*Mozart*? What a name!' Mozart, the boy genius, was one of Ian's heroes. 'Just think, if we'd found him last year in Dublin, he might have ended up being called Metallica. Anyway, why didn't I get a chance to name the kitten?' I complained, as I grabbed some carrot cake. 'After all, I saved him from M.'

'That dog's a nutter.' Ian hadn't forgiven M for climbing onto his bed, then up onto a shelf where his violin case was open and empty. He'd found M sitting in it with a *Go on punk, make my day* expression on his face. When he tried to tip him out, M had leapt at him and sunk his teeth into his right arm. You need two good arms to play the violin I understand.

'He defends his territory. It's the wolf in him,' I explained, not for the first time.

'Do me a favour. It's the crazy in him,' retorted Ian.

'*Sshh*. You'll wake up Mozart.' Mum could scarcely leave the kitten alone. She was all gooey, having found someone to fuss over.

When Dad came in he put up a show of resistance, but we could all tell it wasn't going to last. 'I've got to the time in my life where I want fewer dependants, not more,' he objected, but he was already holding Mozart on his lap. The kitten was growing bolder by the minute. When it was on the kitchen table, it'd venture to the side and peer under to see if it could clamber down.

With Dad in a good mood, I opened my plan of attack. As we ate in the kitchen, I made sure he saw me reading an article in a magazine. Only it was Ian who paid some attention. 'Let's have a butchers.' He leaned over and grabbed the magazine. The article was about Tiger Woods. I let Ian get away with taking it. 'Finking of taking up golf?' he asked.

Thank you, Bruv.

'Not me. It says in that article that golf is extremely good exercise for the older man.' It didn't, but I was relying on nobody bothering to check. Ian threw the magazine down on the table. I reckon he only took it so he could say *give us a butchers*. You don't have to be born within the sound of Bow Bells to know that *butchers* is cockney rhyming slang: butcher's hook – look. I mean, Ian's college isn't even in east London! The closest he'd ever get to cockney slang was when his plane flew over east London before landing at Heathrow.

Dad leaned over and looked at the pictures in the magazine. 'Thinking of having a go, Dad?' I asked.

'What, *me*?' He seemed pleased with the idea, but he always liked to be persuaded.

'You'd be a natural,' I assured him. He looked a bit doubtful. 'Sure, you would. You've got the same physique as Tiger Woods.' That is, he had two arms and two legs.

'It would be good exercise for you.' Mum looked down at her figure, and then took another helping of pasta.

'Some of the fellas at work play, but I wouldn't want to embarrass myself.'

'Tell you what …' I'd been waiting for this moment, 'I'll go out with you, if you want. Have a bash, too.'

'*Bash* will be the right word,' chipped in Ian. 'There won't be a pheasant left standing if you're let loose with a golf club.'

'Are you saying I lack finesse?' I thought I was using some at that very moment, but couldn't point that out.

Ian grinned. 'Davy, mate, it took you a month to learn how to open the French windows.'

I let this go because Dad was looking thoughtful. He had taken the bait.

Unfair!

Joe, Abbas and I were walking around the school grounds at lunchtime when Frazier sauntered up with some of his cronies. 'Your sister chucked Sullivan, then?'

'None of your business who my sister's going out with. What sort of perv are you?' I retorted. Joe and Abbas lined up beside me. I screwed up my crisp packet and threw it at Frazier's feet.

'Yeah, it's got nothing to do with you!' said Joe.

Frazier grinned. 'Trouble in Paradise?' His friends hung back. They couldn't take Joe, Abbas and me and they knew it. Frazier backed away and was well out of kicking distance when he shouted, 'Just wondering why you've been dropped from the team.' Then he turned tail and ran off with his friends.

I was off the A team? I'd scored every game! I'd run faster, tackled more than anyone else. I was *out*? No way! We went to the notice board where teams were posted, to make sure Frazier wasn't just winding me up, but he was right: my name was in the B team list.

'Sullivan's put Cahill in your spot. He hasn't scored a try this season!' exclaimed Abbas. 'And he runs like a girl.'

'Bloody Sullivan,' I muttered.

'But why? Helen hasn't chucked him, has she?' asked Joe, unable to keep the hope out of his voice. When we'd lived in Highfield Road, he'd been a frequent visitor and had stared at Helen more than at my multi-channel TV.

'No, unfortunately. She hasn't got the sense,' I complained. The injustice got to me. I deserved my place on the A team, whatever Frazier and his cronies said. And now I didn't even have that. All thanks to Sullivan. All through Maths class I tried to think of a way to get back my place. Even if I went to the headmaster, he wouldn't do anything about it because whatever Sullivan said, went: with his international caps for Ireland, he was untouchable. Anyway, I couldn't really see myself explaining my sister's love life to the headmaster. That would be like explaining rap lyrics to Mum. The injustice was plain. The Court of Human Rights should deal with this sort of thing, but there was nothing I could do.

My great-uncle Albert won a medal during the war. I only found out about it after he had died. He must have been brave to win the George Cross. You've got to stick up for what you believe in. Stick up for what's right. Trouble is, they don't give you medals for it in my world.

History lesson was last period. Sullivan was *still* going on about the French Revolution. How long could a revolution last, for God's sake? He was pacing up and down the room – a sure sign of trouble. Me, I didn't say a word. Couldn't have been quieter, though when he said that '*Liberty, equality, fraternity*' was the cry of the revolutionaries, I couldn't keep the sneer off my face.

He juddered to a halt in front of me. 'You have something to say, Stirling?' I shook my head. He wasn't getting me that easily. 'Come now! What part of *liberty*, *equality*, *fraternity* do you disagree with?' He'd moved from my desk and gone to a pile of papers in his briefcase. I hoped I was off the hook, then saw he'd taken out my *'Why I must concentrate at all times'* essay. I'd prefer to be talking about *liberty*, *equality*, *fraternity*.

'They could have made it easier,' I said. 'Just shouted *fairness*. That's all that's needed – fairness.' Abbas was looking at me as if I'd just jumped off a tall bridge into a dry river. The rest of the class gaped. News of my demotion from the A team had spread fast. They all knew I was having a go at Sullivan.

He knew it too. 'You seem to have something to say, Stirling, so say it.'

'Why am I off the A team?' I asked. No *sir*. He didn't deserve a *sir*.

'This is History. Keep that for rugby.'

I leapt up, indignant. 'You said I should say what I had to say!'

'Sit down.' There was menace in his voice.

I stayed standing.

'Sit down.'

We were glaring at each other. I wanted to deck him. He looked as if he wanted to deck me. The other boys in the class were swivelling around from him to me as if it was a tennis match. Abbas' eyes were wide like saucers and I could read a message there: *you can't win.*

I sat down, noisily and untidily, giving the bag at my feet a kick. Sullivan took one final look at my essay, scrunched it into a ball and chucked it in the waste bin. Then, talking in a lighter tone than usual, he got back to the French Revolution. The tension in the room eased. I didn't look at him for the rest of the class, spending most of the time scowling and staring out the window onto the rugby pitches. Sullivan left me alone. Sometimes my friends risked looking back at me. Joe caught my eye and shook his head as if to say, *that was close, very close.*

I thought, it isn't over. Not yet.

Second nutty neighbour

'**W**here's M?'

I was in the kitchen and had the first bun in my mouth, but M hadn't run up to greet me since I'd come in from school. Mum had no idea where he was – she only had time for the kitten and its 'cute antics'.

I ran through the house, checking the sorts of places he liked to hide when he had a biscuit to guard (like we wanted it!), but I couldn't find him. He wasn't in the garden either. Maybe he didn't like the scent of cat everywhere. I got his lead. If he thought he was getting a walk, he'd creep out from wherever he was hiding. No luck, no sign of him. I threw my coat back on and grabbed my mobile. 'I'm going to look for him. Text me if he turns up,' I yelled.

I scoured the lane. I'd heard of farmers shooting stray dogs in the country. M wasn't wearing a collar because his hair always got entangled in it, so I only put one on him when I took him for a walk. But with his long, sleek coat, surely even culchies would know he wasn't a stray?

When it was clear he wasn't in the lane, I climbed into the field, calling his name. There was a lot of long grass and once I thought I saw him in the distance, but it turned out to be a plastic bag. I'd been out for over an hour when I heard his bark. I followed the noise into the lane we'd walked along the day before, where the natives had been so 'friendly'. M was nowhere to be seen.

I called out his name again and suddenly Baseball Cap emerged from his wreck of a bungalow. He didn't look any friendlier than he had the day before. I made a show of getting out my phone and calling home. I reckoned it might be safer to let Baseball Cap know that somebody knew where I was. He just kept staring at me. What was with these people?

Just as I was about to walk away, he called out, 'Here, boy, you.'

I turned back. 'Yeah?'

'Why are you always sneaking about around here? You're not from around here. Another blow-in, aren't you? I'm a working man, you know. Need a bit of peace and quiet and here's you, shouting and roaring out of you. What in God's name is "M" anyway?'

I matched his sneer with one of my own. 'That's my dog's name. I can't find him.'

'Dog's name, is it. You cityfolk have queer ways, that's for sure.' That was rich coming from him!

I was in no mood for politeness. 'Well, at least I know how to be friendly instead of just rude.'

He looked at me like I was the one who was crazy. 'What do you mean by that?'

'Last time I saw you, you gave me a two-fingered salute and I didn't appreciate it.'

He stared at me like he didn't believe me. 'I don't know what's up with you, boy. I've only ever waved at you, nothing else. Cheeky.' He walked off.

I'd had enough of this madness. I headed back to *The Haven* to see if my stupid dog had decided to put in an appearance yet.

No sign of M at home, so I went back to the laneway and went on looking. I was nearly past the last bungalow when I saw a face staring out at me from the window. It was my best chance. I decided to call at the door and ask whether the face at the window had seen M. It seemed so easy as I walked up the path, but after I'd knocked, I began to have my doubts. Nobody answered, even though I was sure there had been a face at the window a moment ago. I was being watched by more than Baseball Cap, I was sure. Ballykreig has more than its fair share of idiots: wasn't there meant to be just one per village? If Mum and Dad got out more, they'd find plenty of reasons to move back to Dublin, double-quick.

There was a sign swinging in the wind – *The Belfry* – a weird name for a bungalow. There was no doorbell, so I grabbed hold of the heavy knocker in the middle of the door and hammered away, hoping the owner of the staring face would get the message that I wasn't going to give up any time soon. Eventually, the door opened and I was looking at a small, wiry old man.

'Sorry to bother you …' I began. His face was expressionless, as if he didn't understand what I was saying. Another one! I was trying to find the right words when M came bounding down the hallway towards me. He ran straight past the old man and jumped up at me. I caught him. He was so pleased to see me that he wouldn't stay still. He licked my face and wriggled about.

The old man spoke. 'This your dog, then?' It sounded like a trick question. What had M been up to? Had he chased sheep? Was there a heap of decapitated chickens lying in one of the sheds at the bottom of the garden?

I hesitated. I couldn't get away with saying, 'Dog? Mine? No, never seen it before.' After all, I was holding a dog's lead and M's tail was wagging so vigorously it looked as if he would take off. And he was still licking my face. So I said, 'Err, I know the brother of the person it belongs to.'

'Do you now?'

'Yes, I do.' Well, I did. Ian was the brother of the owner and I certainly knew him.

Anyway, who was this old fella to keep my dog locked up in his house? I knew people stole pedigree dogs and I wasn't about to have M taken by the Village of the Damned. 'I'd prefer if you didn't take my dog inside your home. I spent ages looking for him and I was worried. I'd rather you left him alone. So, I'll be taking him now, thanks.'

I turned and walked away, leaving the old guy standing there with his mouth open. I kept hold of M, not wanting to take the time to put his collar and lead on him, just in case there was a band of pedigree dog thieves inside the bungalow. I'd spent one rainy Sunday watching *A Hundred and One Dalmatians*, so I knew a thing or two about this.

When we were at the gate, I turned. The old man had gone back inside, but Baseball Cap was standing in front of his tumbledown house, watching. I raised two fingers to him, the same way he'd done to me the day before, and decided that any other residents of Nutters Lane probably deserved the same. Still with M in one arm, I raised the other in the air and jerked two fingers. 'Thanks for nothing!' I yelled into the eerie country silence.

That's when she appeared, coming around the corner with those golf clubs in her hand. It was too late to turn my two-fingered salute into a friendly wave. I replayed that moment a hundred times. Every time it was like being kicked in the gut. She stopped, stared at me, then walked on, leaving me gaping. So that was that. I was better off when she thought I was simple-minded!

I slouched home, not even wanting to talk to M. No one at home seemed to register how long we'd been gone. Mum was still crooning over Mozart. 'Did Dad call you?' she asked.

'No, why?'

'He's got a surprise for you.'

'Surprise or shock?'

Mum and Dad are usually plodding and predictable, typical parents, really, but just when I am lulled into a false sense of security they do something spontaneous and crazy. Look at their decision last year to sell our house and buy two next door to each other.

Mum wouldn't tell me what the surprise was, but she promised I'd be pleased. I waited nervously for Dad to come home. When I heard his car come up the driveway, I looked out and saw him lugging a set of golf clubs out of the boot.

He had a grin on his face. 'Look at these, Davy. I bought them in my lunch hour. Fancy coming up the range?'

Would she be up the range? I wasn't keen to meet her.

'I've got loads of homework.'

His face fell. 'This is a transformation, isn't it? You usually do that in the car. What's the matter? Don't fancy your chances against your old dad? Worried I might be better than you?'

'In your dreams!' We were at the golf range within ten minutes. As soon as we got there, I had a good look around, but the place was empty.

We each got a hundred balls out of the machine, went into adjacent bays and started hitting. I used a number 7 iron and my first hit had the ball sailing towards the two hundred-yard line. From watching the professionals on TV (never let anyone tell you TV isn't educational), I'd worked out that the swing was meant to be smooth, the legs steady, the strength coming from the arms. After I'd hit about fifty balls, I looked over at Dad to see how he was getting on. He was scowling at his feet. I went around to see what was up.

'How are you getting on?'

'There's something wrong with these balls. I think we've been given *putting* balls by mistake. They just won't go into the air.' Staring intimidatingly down at the ball, Dad scooped it up. The ball plopped down ten feet away. I grabbed his club. 'This is not a hurley,' I told him. I could see he was going to need some tuition: Remedial Golf.

'First, let's get your stance right.' I squared him up and tried to straighten his S-shaped back. It became a C. 'STRAIGHTEN UP! Legs like so, then you're going to swing the club … but not this club …' I took the club from his hands. 'This is your putter.' I went and got the 7 iron. 'This one you swing with, that one you putt with.' We had left Mum at home introducing Mozart to a cat litter and I realised I was talking in the same sort of voice.

'Look, I'll show you.' I took the iron from him. He stood right behind me. 'Farther back, Dad. I'm going to swing this club.' I demonstrated. 'I could have your head off if you stand there. Now, I look down at the ball so I know where it is …' – believe me, you need to explain the basics to some people. I've seen this man play darts; he hasn't worked out that the idea is to aim for the dartboard – '… then look up and swing.'

A sharp cracking noise and the ball again flew high into the air and landed by the two hundred-yard sign.

'Now you have a go.'

Dad took the iron and got into position. His shoulders were still hunched, but I decided to let that go. I placed a ball down. 'Look at it.' Sullivan had us doing visualisation exercises, so we envisaged scoring tries, but all I wanted at this stage was Dad to remember where the ball was that he was trying to hit. 'Now swing!'

Dad's arms came up, he went boss-eyed and made strange, irregular movements with his legs and arms. The club brushed against the top of the ball and it tricked a few inches, but as Dad let the club flop, it caught the ball again and drove it against the back fence where I was standing. Instinctively I dodged out of the way and covered my head. He'd got a minus score: he'd driven the ball *minus* five feet. He looked forlorn, so I decided not to joke that he might do better if he turned around and tried to hit the ball backwards. I watched him try to hit another five balls, but then despair overcame me and I went back to my own bay. The way Dad was moving when he tried to hit a ball reminded me of the way he looked when he was on the dancefloor – everything was moving, but without pattern or purpose. And forget rhythm!

When we'd finished – I had hit the hundred balls; I'm not sure what Dad did with his – we drove out of the golf range in silence. I couldn't blame him for being demoralised. Fortunately, only I had witnessed his performance, but surely he wouldn't want to be seen thrashing away like that? I wondered if you could be sent off a golf course, like in rugby. Imagine, Dad escorted off the greens 'for bringing the game into disrepute'.

Q. What do you say to the inflatable man on an inflatable golf course with a pin?

A. You have let the game down. You have let yourself down …

My sad old Dad. He was bad, very bad. Me, I was good, very good.

The importance of etiquette

'**N**ot in here, David!'
'Why not?' What's a sitting room for if not a little gentle putting? I reckoned the carpet had about the same friction as grass. Dad had bought a putting machine that made a satisfying noise when the ball went in. I guess he was trying to buy his way into the game. Added to his golf clubs and golf bag, he'd acquired a putting machine, golf trousers, golf jumpers and golf shoes. He was even kitted out with those socks with little diamond patterns on the side. He looked the part, walked the walk, talked the talk.

When Mum asked him how much it had all cost, he muttered something about getting a 'great deal'. Could the salesman see him coming! Finally he'd admitted he had got a discount of €300 and Mum had shrieked, 'If that was the discount, what was the price?' But Dad wouldn't tell her the percentage discount, knowing she'd get me to work out the price.

Maths Problem

If one gullible man walks into a golf shop and is duped into thinking he's getting a good deal when a salesman tells him he's getting a discount of €300, and that discount is X percent, how much would an even bigger idiot be prepared to pay?

So far, I didn't have any golf stuff of my own, but I was the one putting six out of seven balls. Let me loose on Crazy Golf at Bray and I'd be cleaning up!

Mum didn't see it like that. 'Golf's an outdoor game, David. Why don't you go up the driving range?'

'This is putting. See? The ball doesn't leave the ground.' That's how most of Dad's shots ended up. That, or a clump of grass flew into the air. It's called a *divot*. I was jenning up on golf lingo by watching Sky Sports. Mozart had squeezed into the room with Mum. The kitten was getting bolder by the day, venturing out of the kitchen and utility area, exploring. When I hit the ball, it pounced on it. M immediately pounced on the kitten and the two of them rolled around the room. I prized them apart, but Mozart threw himself at M. I had to separate them again and give the kitten to Mum to hide in her apron pocket.

'Here, watch this.' I putted the next ten putts, even with the distraction of M going for the ball each time. Mum watched. Ten out of ten. I waited for praise. 'Outside,' was all she said before she left. If there isn't a degree in it, my parents just aren't interested. Tiger Woods' dad had him golfing when he was three years old! He didn't have to worry about how to get his hands on a set of golf clubs.

Ian sailed in. 'Wanna practice,' he said, sitting down at the grand piano. 'Shove off.'

'Shove off yourself. I *am* practicing.' I lobbed a ball at

him. 'This is called *chipping*.'

He let out a girly little yelp. 'Do that again and I'll …'

I did it again. Ian groaned and I thought I might have overdone it, but then I realised that, with his batlike ears, he'd heard Mum talking to a visitor in the kitchen.

'*Brendan*,' he hissed.

Sullivan had once tried to engage Ian in friendly conversation. He thinks everyone follows sport. And as he'd started working at St Joe's after Ian had left, he had no idea what he was up against. He asked Ian what he thought of Manchester United's chances in the Cup. By the time he had explained who 'Man U' were and which Cup he meant, he realised he was unlikely to get an informed opinion. He didn't ask me, of course. He never forgot I was *Stirling*, one of his wingers. That was okay with me. I never forgot he was my rugby coach and History teacher.

I hesitated. It was Sunday, three days since I'd stood up to him in class. We hadn't even had a rugby practice yet. I still had the full humiliation of practicing with the B team to look forward to. I heard tinkly laughter coming from the kitchen. Maybe I should stay where I was, wait until he was out of the way? But this was *my* territory, not his. He was in Stirling Country now.

I left Ian playing something fast and furious on the piano and went into the kitchen. I was greeted by the sight of Sullivan with his arm around Helen, all lovey smiles. Pass the sick bucket, please! Mum was trying to persuade them to have a cake. I put my hand over the plate she was holding in front of them and scooped up a couple.

'Thanks. Don't mind if I do.'

Helen scowled, but she watches what she says in front of boyfriends. She likes them to think she's sweet. Sweet as a scorpion.

Sullivan nodded in my direction. I nodded back, my mouth full of cake. M trotted in behind me and sniffed around them. Sullivan slammed one of his enormous hands down fast on M's back and ruffled his coat. According to Helen, he'd grown up with dogs and knew how to handle them. He was a country boy and thought every dog was like a working dog, so he acted as if he were a shepherd and M was rounding up a flock of sheep. I don't think so! M growled and bared his teeth, but just when it was turning interesting, Mum said, 'Davy! Put M in the garden.'

Reluctantly, I dragged M out just as Dad came in from the garden. 'Hello Brendan!' he said cheerily. Though he doesn't rate my rugby, he's impressed by Sullivan's international career. He's always getting it into the conversation.

'Mr Stirling.' Sullivan flashed a smile. 'All well with you?'

'Fine, fine, just, er …' Dad was struggling to find some common interest, '… just taken up a new hobby actually.'

'Sport,' I corrected him. 'Golf's a sport. Restyling your hair, basket-weaving, crochet work, they're hobbies.'

'What are your plans today?' Mum asked quickly.

'We're out to lunch,' said Sullivan.

'That's a permanent condition with you!' I said promptly. I was the only one to laugh. That's good enough for me.

Sullivan was still standing. I sat down on one of the six seats around the big kitchen table. 'Why don't you sit down?' I said, pulling out a chair. He glared at me. 'Sit down,' I repeated.

'Yes, where are my manners? Do sit down, Brendan,' added Mum. I grinned.

'Sit down,' I said again, fixing him with a look. 'Sit down.' I was enjoying this. I gave him a look that I hoped said, *You can't win.*

Reluctantly he sat down. I gave him a wonderful smile, then stood up. I knew he wanted to throttle me, but it was worth it. He took a minute to recover. Then he said to Dad, 'Golf. So, where are you planning to join?'

'Dimbrook. It's just down the road.'

Sullivan whistled. 'Tough. It's very popular. There's probably a waiting list for membership.'

'Dead man's shoes,' I explained. Sullivan was trying to squeeze me out of the conversation, but I wasn't having any of it. 'Dad's got to wait till some member dies. Mind you, since Helen drives past the entrance everyday, the chances are well good.'

Dad gave me a look. 'I'm being proactive,' he said grandly. He'd been calling in at Dimbrook's public bar and coming back smelling of Guinness.

'Play of seven myself,' said Sullivan, smugly. I glared. Another thing he was good at.

'Dad's put his work first. Isn't that what you said the other day, Dad? That you wouldn't have dreamed of taking it up when you were younger because you have different priorities?'

'Err … what do you think of our chances in the Six Nations this year, Brendan?' Dad asked, clearly put out to have his words thrown back at him in front of Sullivan.

'Yeah, Brendan,' I asked in pally fashion, leaning on the work surface, 'what'da ya think?'

For a second his eyes bulged to hear me call him Brendan and then he said, 'Strong squad. Naughton's playing like a demon! What a star!'

Dad agreed, nodding vigorously. Helen was nibbling on single crumbs of a cake and Mum was fussing with Mozart while this farce of male bonding was going on.

'I reckon Naughton should be scrapped.'

Dad gaped at me. 'But he scored two tries last Saturday.'

'Yeah, throw him off.'

'And his kicking is superb,' objected Dad.

'B team stuff. What do you think, *Brendan*?' I guess he'd worked out that I hadn't told my family what he'd done. They didn't know I'd been relegated to the B team. He managed a grin. 'I think … I think …' He stood up and turned to Helen. 'I think if we don't go now, we'll miss our restaurant reservations.'

'Don't let us keep you.' I gave him a little wave and a smile. 'Byeee, Brendan.'

Ian waited until Sullivan had driven away with Helen before coming out of the sitting room. 'Wot an ape!' he said. 'Fick as two short planks.'

'Thick as the trunk of a tree sandwiched between two short planks,' I agreed.

'How can that be?' asked Mum indignantly. 'He teaches at St Joseph's.'

I explained. 'It *be* because he played rugby for Ireland. St Joe's would have him on the staff whatever. He could have a walnut for a brain. Don't blame me if my history stinks. I'm being seriously misinformed. When was the Easter Rising? Some time around Christmas?'

Dad shook his head. 'You were talking utter rubbish about Naughton. Sometimes I wonder what you're on.'

'Indignation sprinkled with righteous anger,' I told him. I picked a cherry off the top of a cake. 'Topped off with some nice juicy revenge.'

'Whatever about all that nonsense, I've got some news about my application,' Dad told me. 'The waiting list is closed at the moment.'

'*Closed*! You mean you've got to wait before you get to *wait*?'

'On a conservative estimate, it could be ten years before I get in.'

'*Ten years!* But I'll be in my twenties by then. I wanted to be playing by next weekend.' But Dad didn't look as disappointed as I'd expected.

'There is … a loophole.' Dad loves loopholes – plugging them when he is at work and going through them when he isn't.

'So?'

'There are vacancies in the youth section.' Dad was looking everywhere but at me. Basically, he was telling me that *I* could get into the golf club, but *he* couldn't. The idea was killing him.

'Hard luck. Still, you weren't making much progress, were you? Can I have your clubs?'

'Not so fast! And what do you mean, *not making much progress*? I hit that ball nearly a hundred yards, you said so yourself.'

'Into the car park, Dad. The *car park*.'

'Be that as it may ...' Dad was having difficulty getting something out, '... as far as membership of Dimbrook is concerned, I can play if you're a member.'

'Okay.' More than okay. I imagined Dad, standing waiting, all dressed up in his golfing trousers, his golfing jumper, his special golfing socks, needing *me*. I would be a member; he would be my guest.

'So, how about it?' asked Dad.

'Well ... there's one problem.'

'What's that?'

'We can't both play with the same set of golf clubs, can we? It's not allowed. The etiquette of golf doesn't allow it.'

'Since when were you into *etiquette*?'

Since it got me my own golf clubs.

'That's the way it is,' I said firmly. 'No golf clubs. No membership. No chance.'

'Alright. I'll buy you some.'

Result! 'A full set?'

'If you must.'

Oh, I think I must. 'Pings?'

'Pings! Are you mad? Surely you could make do with some second-hand ones?'

'Sorry. No can do.' I wanted *her* to see me with the best set of clubs on the market. 'Brand new Pings,' I insisted.

The sound of Dad over a barrel was more beautiful than any music. 'Go on then.'

'Great. Thanks Dad.' When the kitten came up to me, I picked him up. Mozart. He wasn't the only genius about!

'Everybody's mad
but thee and me ...'

I dragged myself and my kit off the bus. I'd caught it with seconds to spare. I hadn't even had time for a shower after rugby. Training with the B team had been the hell I had expected. My new team-mates were determined to show they were as tough as an A team player, so I'd had more than my fair share of booting and winding. There was a long scratch down one arm and the seeping blood was cold against my skin. I'd washed my face, but the mud had dried on my legs. A crappy day all round.

I wanted chocolate. I had just enough energy to make it to the village shop. The notice on the door said *Closed*. I looked up at the shop sign: *McDonnell's 24/7*. What the hell was it doing closed if it was a 24/7? I rattled the door, but it was definitely locked. As I turned to go, I bumped into the red-haired girl. 'Sorry,' I mumbled. The look she gave me wasn't unfriendly, so I was hoping she'd forgotten our last encounter.

This was my chance. She was carrying two golf clubs again, so I said, 'Off to the golf range?' As soon as the words were spoken, I wished them back again. *She was carrying two golf clubs.* Where else did I think she was going? Fishing? Ballet class? Talk about stating the obvious!

But she gave me a smile and said, 'Yeah, I'm a member up at Dimbrook. You play?'

'Going to,' I said quickly – definitely going to now.

'Okay, see you.'

'Yeah, see you.'

I ran home. The dried blood didn't seem to matter anymore. I wanted to get my hands on my own set of golf clubs and start practicing.

I started on Dad the first chance I got. 'So, when are we going out for my golf clubs?'

'Oh, you've not forgotten then,' he said gloomily.

'No chance,' I assured him.

'Well, how about Saturday, after rugby. Do you have a game?'

'No.' The B team wasn't playing till the week after, but Dad didn't keep up with my schedule, so he hadn't worked out that I'd been dropped.

'Saturday then.'

'If we're going into Dublin, can Joe and Abbas come back with me?' I could go to the range with my new clubs, and if she was there, I'd have proper back-up instead of Dad doing his comic turn.

'And you're going to mow the lawn twice a week all summer?' Dad asked.

'Won't Ian be back again by then? Shouldn't he take a turn?'

'Ian has to be careful about his hands.' It's like I'm expendable! But I wanted those clubs more than ever. I nodded.

'And you'll build that rockery?' Dad was determined to get his money's worth of jobs out of me.

'I'll need some gloves and golfing trousers.'

'The rockery?'

'For three gloves, some golfing trousers, shoes and some practice balls.'

'For two gloves, no trousers, shoes and I've bought some balls already.'

'For three gloves, trousers and shoes.'

'A deal, but don't go for those flashy two-tone shoes. They cost a fortune.'

As if!

Saturday came and I got my Ping golf clubs. And guess what? The shop gave Dad a discount of €200. What a bargain! Then we picked up Joe and Abbas.

'Will Helen be at home?' asked Joe.

'What's it to you? When we go to Abbas' for tea, you don't ask if his sister is going to be there,' I said.

'She's six.'

'So, lads ...' Dad interrupted, with what he imagined was his jovial, fatherly voice, 'how's the *craic*? All well at school?'

There was an uncomfortably long silence before Abbas answered, 'Yes, thank you, Mr Stirling. All is going very well indeed.' Then he artfully got Dad off that hot topic by telling him about his summer holiday back in Sri Lanka. Loads of his family were still there and some of them had been caught up in the tsunami at Christmas, but fortunately none of them had been killed. I'd like to go there one day, to see what it's really like.

As we drove through Ballykreig, I could see Joe and Abbas were wondering what the hell there was to do out here. It was the first time they'd seen the place. We sat in the kitchen, sampling Mum's cakes and watching M and the kitten. Mozart was racing round, pursued by M. When he got within striking distance, M pounced and they started rolling round together, one moving ball of fur.

'*Wow!* A cat and dog fight,' said Joe.

'No.' I'd seen it all before. As Mozart settled in, he and M spent more and more of their time play-fighting. I was starting to suspect that Mozart believed he was a dog. 'The kitten hasn't got her claws out and look ...' M was shaking Mozart '... M isn't biting.'

It was quite a display. We all watched as Mozart made a break for it, jumped up onto the table and then, with the advantage of height, launched himself onto M. The double ball of fur rolled around the kitchen.

'I thought cats and dogs were enemies,' said Abbas.

'Nobody told the kitten,' I said.

I led them up to my attic room. I suddenly realised how big it was, remembering how small the bedrooms were in Highfield Road. Even with two vast mahogany wardrobes in one corner and my double bed under one of the windows, there's still masses of space. I could practice putting up there if the floor was more even. And it looks even bigger because there's no ceiling – you can look right up into the roof. Joe jumped up, grabbed hold of one of the beams and started swinging. 'Magic!' he yelled.

Abbas went over to my computer station and started sorting through the games littered about. At his house, he had to keep everything hidden away from his little brothers and sisters. Sometimes he came to school with wax crayon all over his homework. At least, in my family, any crayoning vandalism had been done by me!

When Joe had had enough of gymnastics, he swung down and went to the window, scanning the view. 'You can see for miles,' he marvelled. Abbas joined us.

I pointed. 'Fields, trees, fields, trees.' I'd stared out of that window often enough, searching for something interesting. No chance. I'd once watched a black bin-liner swirl in the wind, around and around until it got caught in a tree. Even the sky took up more space in the country.

I was impatient, ready to get to the range, to hold my new clubs.

'And no traffic,' said Abbas.

'That's because there's hardly any people,' I explained. 'Just a few very disturbed individuals.'

'Still, you've got all this space,' said Abbas.

'And peace and quiet,' added Joe.

'Davy! *Quickly!*' Mum was calling.

I leapt down the stairs followed by my friends. I knew it was an M-induced panic by Mum's shout. No one was in the kitchen, but the back door was open. Outside, Sullivan was backed up against his car with M hanging off his arm. Sullivan looked mighty scared. He was waving his free hand about while M moved up and down on his other arm as if he was doing benchpresses. I could see Joe and Abbas delighting in seeing Sullivan like this, they were struggling not to laugh.

One thing I know: a single dog can't be biting two people at once. I grabbed M round his middle and threw him down, backing off before he could go for my feet. He yapped in the long grass for a while, then skulked away to sit under a tree, head down, eyes open, brooding.

Mum rushed over to see if Sullivan was injured. He wasn't because he had on the wax jacket he wears when he's watching rugby from the sidelines. M's teeth hadn't even penetrated the material.

'I'm so sorry, Brendan,' Mum was saying. 'He's very highly strung.'

I reckoned I was owed a *thank you*, but I knew I wouldn't get it, particularly with Abbas and Joe there. 'You just have to know how to handle him,' I said resentfully. Sullivan just shook his head. He didn't like the audience, so we were spared a lecture about how dogs should be disciplined.

'He was fighting a kitten, terrorising it. I tried to part them,' he explained, dusting himself down.

'You mean, the kitten that shares his basket?' I asked. At school we're given all sorts of guff about *judging by the evidence*. You get % in History if you don't *verify* what you say, but here was Sullivan jumping to conclusions. To prove my point, Mozart had raced after M and they were chasing round the garden.

'Davy, take M for a walk with your friends,' Mum said, giving me a look.

'But–' I objected

'*But nothing.* I'm sure they'd like a walk in the country-side, wouldn't you boys?' She didn't get an answer, but I had to go and get the lead while Mum fussed over Sullivan as if he'd lost an arm.

'Which way do you want to go?' I asked Joe and Abbas as we made our way through the gates of *The Haven* and down the hill. 'That way, towards the one and only village shop, or that way, towards the old git who stole M?' They shrugged. I didn't blame them. It's all desolate wilderness whichever way we go.

'I wanted to take you up the range,' I complained. 'We could've tried out my new clubs.' They decided to resist the excitement of the village shop and wanted to see the shantytown bungalow and where the old fella who'd taken M lived.

'I call it Nutters Lane,' I told them.

'Why?' asked Joe. 'You said earlier there were "disturbed individuals". Anyone we should know about?'

I let M off the lead so he could wander.

'Well,' I said, 'the country is naturally full of culchies, and brain cells are hard to come by in these here parts.' Joe started laughing. 'I met this one old guy, really strange, and he gave me a two-fingered hello – and I hadn't even said anything. And there's another old guy who has an unhealthy interest in M – I think he's a dog thief and I have to keep a close eye on him.' I was really warming to my theme now. 'And of course we have the village idiot, who runs the shop and thinks 24/7 means twenty-four random hours in any given week.'

Joe was laughing hard now. 'Are there visiting hours at the asylum? I want to see some weirdos. Take us to Nutters Lane.'

Abbas was not laughing. He looked from me to Joe and then said, 'My father says, be sure before you judge. You know, he had an important job in Sri Lanka, but here some people see only a man with a different colour skin.'

I was quiet.

'Some people, they see me and they say...' he put on a patronising tone, '... do you speak English? And then they ask, "When are you going home?" And they don't mean Highfield Road.'

I looked at Joe. I didn't know what to say. I looked down and kicked a stone along the road. 'I was just kidding, Abbas.'

He didn't look convinced. 'I'm just saying, give them a chance.'

I smiled at him, 'My great-uncle Albert, you know, the one I told you about, he won a medal in the War. He had a saying: *Everyone's mad but thee and me, and thou art a bit strange.*'

Abbas laughed. 'We're all different.'

We walked on. When we reached Nutters Lane, we saw

the girl with the red hair sitting on the wall in front of the bungalows. With my friends there, I felt bolder. 'Hi!' I called, as if she and I were friends. She jumped off the wall and came towards us. She was smiling down at M. I was ready for a girly, *Does he bite?* but she bent down and started stroking M, and not the way Sullivan did it, but gently, as if she knew about dogs.

'Isn't he cute?' That's undeniable. 'What's his name?' she asked.

'His pedigree name's Man of Honour.' M was enjoying the attention. 'He's not usually friendly to strangers.'

She bent down further so her face was level with M's, took his giant ears in her hands and said in a pally voice to him, not to me, 'Why should you be?' M was wagging his tail furiously. Joe and Abbas were staring at her. 'Sheltie puppy, is he?'

'No. He's a Papillion.' I pointed to M's big butterfly ears.' *Papillion* is the French word for butterfly,' I explained. 'And that black spot on his head's meant to be like a butterfly, too.'

'Not often you see the breed around here,' she said. That was a bigger understatement than me saying M wasn't friendly to strangers. I'd never seen another Papillion in the region, let alone the neighbourhood.

'We got him in Cork. That's the nearest breeder.' This conversation was going well. I was telling her stuff she didn't know. 'I had to search the Internet to find the sort of dog I wanted. Mum had said I could have one only if it was small. He's a mighty midget.' I didn't want her to think he was like a pink poodle with ribbons in his hair.

'You all new around here?' she asked.

'I am. These are my friends from school, in Dublin. That's Joe and that's Abbas.'

'Hi, enjoying the countryside?' she asked.

'Sure are,' answered Joe, and Abbas nodded enthusiastically.

'The people seem very pleasant,' added Abbas, as if he'd talked to every resident.

'You live in one of these?' I asked, pointing at the bungalows, just as someone called '*Andrea!*' from one of them. So now I knew her name. Andrea.

'Got to go now.' She ran off. We all watched her go. Finally Joe gave an appreciative whistle and said, 'Nice wilderness you've got here, Davy.'

'How did you meet her?' asked Abbas.

'We just met, in the lane.'

'You can't do that in Dublin – talk to a girl just because you pass her in the street.'

It was only after we'd got back home, after we'd tried out my new golf clubs in the grounds of *The Haven* and Joe and Abbas were on the bus back to Dublin that I realised what had happened, what we had seen. I knew her name: Andrea. She'd been friendly to M. More amazing, he had liked her back. But when we'd watched her race away, she'd gone into *The Belfry*. She knew the old dog thief! Perhaps she lived there. Perhaps she'd seen M before, too. And perhaps I had one more nutter to worry about!

The day things changed

The next week, even homework time in the car on the way to school was spent wondering about Andrea and the bungalow called *The Belfry*. Had the old man who lived there just seen M running loose and taken him in to be helpful? Had he been looking out for M's owner? Or was he a dog snatcher who knew only too well that M was a pedigree dog? And if he was, what did that make Andrea? A dog snatcher, too? I'd been pleased the way she had been so friendly to M and he to her, but now I wasn't so sure. Just my luck! One nice-looking girl in the whole of this wilderness and she was involved in some sort of canine smuggling ring. And they were already one step ahead of me – I'd told her M's pedigree name, so now they'd be able to look him up in Kennel Club records and work out how valuable he was.

'What's wrong with you? Has that school stopped giving homework?' Dad broke into my thoughts.

'I'm thinking.'

'Wonders will never cease. I'll have to put a note in my diary,' Dad joked. Then he got suspicious. 'Are you in some sort of trouble? Am I going to have some horrible shock when I see your report card?'

'No!' I was indignant. 'Anyway, I couldn't get away with that, could I? Helen's *boyfriend* would grass me up.'

'*Grass me up?* You're starting to sound like Ian.' But before I got out of the car Dad said, 'How about I pick you up from school and we go straight to the range?'

'Okay, you're on!'

I looked forward to that all day. Every time some loser made a comment about me being in the B team, I'd keep my cool and say to myself, 'New golf clubs. I'm gonna cream it.'

When Dad and I drove back to *The Haven* later that day, we just picked up our golf clubs and went straight off, not even stopping for a snack. My clubs glinted in the sunlight as I took them out of the boot of the car. They looked great. I was going to test out each one of them. 'Turn off your phone, Dad,' I told him, switching off mine. 'Golfing etiquette.' I didn't want any shots interrupted.

There were a couple of old duffers hacking away in the bays, but no sign of Andrea. I wasn't disappointed. I preferred to practice with my new clubs first without being watched. We planned to hit two hundred balls. We each took a bucket of one hundred, but after he had been hacking away for ten minutes or so, Dad came into my bay and dumped his bucket down at my side. 'You use these. I've got backache from all that gardening at the weekend.'

I hit away. My longest drive nearly reached the two hundred-and-fifty-yard marker. Then I started chipping. When I'd finished Dad said, 'You're getting the hang of this.'

'Yeah, I'm ready to have a go on the course. How's my membership application going?'

'I've filled in all the paperwork and handed it in. It's important to be proactive.'

That word again. 'What does *proactive* mean?' I asked. 'Something to do with drinking a lot?'

'I'm oiling the wheels,' he explained.

That's not all that was getting oiled.

'I've been going to the bar at Dimbrook, to get my face known.'

'Sure that's a good idea?' I asked, but I fancied a trip to the clubhouse. 'How about we go together when we've hit these balls?' I suggested.

Dad hesitated. 'It's getting late …'

'Come on, Dad, practice makes perfect you always told me!' He could have some of his 'wise sayings' back.

I wanted to see inside the clubhouse and get a closer look at the course. I could see some holes from the road, but what I really wanted was to walk around it so I could start envisioning playing it. 'Envisioning' is the technique Sullivan teaches the rugby squad. We make mental pictures of successfully tackling opponents, scoring tries, etc. He calls it *the power of positive thinking*.

Dad took me to the clubhouse. I liked the look of the place. There was a public bar, which we went into, but the members' bar looked better. It had a huge TV with all the channels. I could see it would be a useful bolthole. The barman greeted Dad like he'd seen him before and Dad ordered drinks.

I asked the barman how I could get to walk around the course. 'See one of the committee,' he answered.

Dad asked, 'Mike, who's in charge of the juveniles?'

'That would be old Frank Lynch.'

'Does he decide who gets in?' I asked.

Mike nodded. 'That's how it works. He'll look at your application, might interview you.'

I grimaced. I didn't like the sound of that.

'They're in need of juvenile members. We've got a waiting list as long as your arm for main membership, but it's a different story with the juveniles. We've only got Andy Donaldson who's any good.' I looked around for him. I was the only teenager in the place. He wasn't up the range. He wasn't in the club. How keen could he be? The answer came to me – keen enough to be out on the course.

'Could I have a word with Mr Lynch?' Dad asked. 'Buy him a drink?'

'Doesn't come in as much as he used to. Doesn't live far from here, though. One of the bungalows on the road into the village.'

Nutters Lane!

'He doesn't wear a red baseball cap, does he?' I asked nervously. I didn't stand a cat in hell's chance if that crazy coot was the boss.

'What? Old Frank Lynch!'

'Then he doesn't live in that bungalow with loads of sheds all round it?' I asked.

The barman continued to dry a glass. 'Nah! That's old Declan. He's gone from bad to worse these last few years.'

I was reeling from the news that the person who had my golfing future in his hands lived in Nutters Lane. I heard Mike add, 'We all remember what he did to his wife,' before I asked, 'So where does he live?'

'Frank Lynch lives in the last bungalow before you get into the village.'

'*The Belfry?*'

'Yeah, that's the one.'

I suddenly realised the significance of the name the old git – correction – esteemed committee member had given his home. The Belfry was a famous golf course. I should have realised. Why else would a one-storey building be called that? So this Frank Lynch was the person who decided whether I was in or out. We had already met, and not in the best of circumstances. And if I recalled rightly, I may have been a tad sharp with him. I wondered if he'd connect my name with what happened at his front door, when I'd appeared and taken M away. There was no reason he should, except that newcomers to the area stood out. Any new faces were noticeable around here. We didn't even walk the same as the locals: they rolled along as if the road was moving, not them. I bet I'd been spotted. I bet he'd made the connection. I needed some food to cheer me up, so I reached for the bar menu, but Dad was checking his phone. 'Ten missed calls,' he said. He looked. 'All from home.'

I checked my phone. 'Yeah, me too.'

We skipped food, went straight to the car and headed back in silence, both wondering what could have happened to make Mum call so often. Okay, we were late, but not that late. I kept trying Mum's mobile and the house phone, but there was no answer from either.

We were close to home when Dad drove round a bend and we found ourselves staring at a car in the ditch. It was a yellow Volkswagen. Helen's car. Dad pulled onto the verge and we ran to the car. We didn't have to open a door to look in because the front passenger door had been ripped off. It lay beyond the car, in the ditch. The near side of the car was crumpled in, the bonnet raised, revealing a tangled mass of engine parts. The car was empty. Dad just stood staring at the car, like he was paralysed.

I used the front passenger seat to clamber up onto the roof. I wanted to look over the hedges to see if there was anything beyond on the winding road. I don't know what I expected to see – another car perhaps, or Helen limping along towards *The Haven*. The *limping along* bit was wishful thinking – I could bear to think of Helen with minor injuries, but what if my sister were hurt a lot worse?

My heart thumped. Perhaps she'd already been taken to hospital by ambulance. Perhaps she was dead. She could have been dying in the tangled wreckage while Dad and I were in the clubhouse, or even when we had been at the range, which was almost close enough for us to have heard the crash.

'Nothing,' I shouted to Dad, easing myself down.

'We'll have to go home,' said Dad. I nodded.

We raced home. I was hoping that we'd find Mum putting a few plasters on Helen, but I knew really that the car was a write-off and that must mean Helen had more than cuts and bruises.

I jumped out of the car as Dad slowed down in the driveway and raced through the back door. All seemed normal. M was in his basket and came forward, wagging his tail. Mozart was weaving about on the kitchen table. There was no sign of Mum, Ian, or Helen, but we saw the note soon enough. I grabbed it. It was written in a shaky version of Mum's handwriting:

Helen in Beaumont hospital. Car accident.

No indication of how badly Helen was hurt. We tried Mum's phone again. Then Ian's. 'They must be in the hospital and have turned their phones off,' I guessed. From my frequent visits to Accident and Emergency departments for rugby injuries, I knew phones had to be switched off near medical equipment.

'We're wasting time,' said Dad. 'Let's go.'

Desperately needed: the power of positive thinking

Dad drove towards Dublin with ferocious determination. He took some chances, and we reached the hospital in record time. I kept ringing Mum and Ian, but their phones were still off and the hospital line was constantly engaged. It wasn't just Dad's driving that was furious. I knew he was keeping his worry at bay by being angry.

'I always said Helen needed more driving lessons. I blame the examiner who passed her.' Then he thought of someone else to blame. 'And that Sullivan! Since she met him, she's been rushing about – home from work, then zooming back into Dublin for a date.' Since Helen spent about three hours getting ready for any date, that wasn't actually fair, but I kept quiet.

All I kept thinking was: why had she been taken all the way into Dublin? There were smaller hospitals nearby. It must be because her injuries were so serious she need special attention, special equipment.

When we pulled into the hospital car park, I couldn't wait for Dad to park. As he slowed the car, I opened the door and leapt out. I raced into the reception and asked where Helen Stirling was. The receptionist looked up her name slowly, as if it was routine, which it was for her, I suppose. Dad had parked and was beside me by the time I got an answer. We walked down corridors that smelled of disinfectant and illness at the same time.

We found Ian and Mum in a waiting room. Mum was still wearing her boat-like slippers. She ran up to Dad. I heard him ask, 'How bad?' and strained to hear the answer.

I heard something like *broken bones*, but then Mum spoke so softly I couldn't hear the rest.

'What?' I demanded. 'Where is she? How is she?' I couldn't believe how I felt. Frantic is the best word I can think of. It was seeing the car and then having a long journey knowing nothing, having time to imagine the worst.

'She's in surgery,' Mum said.

'What for?' Dad and I asked together.

'She hit the steering wheel, here.' Mum pointed to her forehead. ' A piece of bone is resting on her brain. They're operating to lift it.'

The meaning of the words hit me. Helen was having brain surgery. That's why she'd been brought to Beaumont.

'Will she be alright?' I asked. I wanted what I knew I couldn't have – a definite *yes*. Mum gave me a little pat on the arm and said, like I was still a baby, 'Alright? Of course she'll be alright!'

Mum started to cry. 'The surgeon who spoke to me said he does this sort of operation often. But there's always a risk …'

Ian rushed up. He had two plastic cups in his hand. He gave one to Mum, thought for a second and handed the second one to Dad.

'You've heard?' he asked. The mock-cockney accent was gone. He looked worried sick but calm, dead calm and I knew I had to stay like that too. Mum looked as if she was close to fainting and Dad was all quivery around the mouth. 'We've just got to wait,' Ian said. We all sat down on a long seat. I leant forward, head down, thinking, making sure I didn't cry. Helen. I wanted her back, just as she was, just as she had been – vain, silly, crazy about one boyfriend or another. *Boyfriend!* I looked up quickly.

'Has anyone told Sullivan?'

Swift looks all round. Mum and Ian had been too busy talking to doctors, then seeing Helen into the operating theatre. No one had given Sullivan a thought. Something changed for me at that moment. Okay I hated the guy, hated the way he was getting at me at school, hated the injustice of losing my place on the A team. Hell, just the weekend before I'd saved him from a mauling from M only to save M's ass! But he was Helen's boyfriend. She spoke about him, *Brendan says this*, *Brendan says that*, as if quoting Holy Scripture. And he had a doelike expression when he looked at her. He needed to know what had happened.

Trouble was, none of us had his phone number. Of course I'd see him at school the next day ... if I went to school. I suddenly saw that life had changed. The old routine was gone. Dad and I wouldn't be stuck on the Long Mile Road tomorrow morning. We'd still be at the hospital. I felt sick to my stomach, thinking of the way things might be by then.

Ian was focusing on how we'd contact Sullivan. He's remarkable, my brother. In ordinary, everyday situations he's useless. It's a miracle he can travel to London and back by himself. When we had seen him off at the airport at the beginning of his first term, I'd prepared myself for a call from Krakow, Delhi, or Brisbane because he'd wandered onto the wrong plane. Then, just when he'd established an unrivalled reputation as a complete airhead, Flimsy McFeeble became sturdier, stronger. He took control and amazed me by holding it all together. 'I'll drive home and find Helen's phone. I reckon it'll be in the car. I'll keep my phone on, so as soon as there's any news, go outside and phone me. Right?'

'Right,' I agreed and before he left we hugged. The Stirlings had to stick together now.

Our long wait started. Even though there was a TV blaring out in the waiting room, I couldn't watch it. We ate crisps and chocolate bars from the vending machine, drank tea that could have been coffee, coffee that could have been tea. It didn't matter. We just had to get through the hours until Helen's operation was over.

As night approached, the hospital became quieter. There was still activity – strong lights burning and the clatter of trolleys, doors bursting open with new casualties who we stared at with morbid interest – but now we kept our voices down, as if we had dim memories of the world outside where sleep came with the night.

I got to thinking about death and the first time I realised, properly realised what it meant. It had been when my great-uncle Albert died. We went over to clear out his house in Waltham Abbey, in England. There were all his familiar things – his old armchair, papers he'd been reading, an old pipe, even a musty smell that belonged to his old house. The antique that had always fascinated me, a ship made out of spun glass in vivid red, white and blue, still stood on a mantelpiece. But Albert was gone. Gone, leaving all his stuff behind him. Death was leaving, without goodbyes. It meant never seeing someone again, never hearing their voice again. Words unsaid, arguments unfinished, a story that comes to an abrupt, shocking finish. I began to shake.

'Are you cold?' whispered Mum. I shook my head.

'You okay?' I asked. She nodded, then crumpled and I put my arm around her. I thought about *the power of positive thinking*. I had to get Mum envisioning Helen better. 'She'll get through this,' I told Mum. I had to give her pictures, real pictures. 'Helen will be sitting up in bed within days. You know how she paints her toenails?' I impersonated Helen in the middle of a grooming session. *'Which colour looks best? This vermillion, or the lavender? This one brings out my skin tones. This one will coordinate with my new top …'* Mum managed a smile.

When I looked up, Sullivan was charging towards us, with Ian following. 'How is she?' he asked.

'We're still waiting,' Dad said. Ian had filled Sullivan in on what was happening, so there was nothing more to add, though when you're that worried about something, you can go round and round, over the same bits again and again. Supposing the brain operation isn't 100% successful and Helen's left with some mental disability? Supposing the bone pushing on her brain changes her? Supposing we get back a different Helen? Supposing the cuts on her face don't heal and she's no longer beautiful? She'd hate that.

'Mum, if Helen doesn't look ... right, will she lose her job?'

Mum didn't answer.

'She'll always be beautiful to me,' Sullivan said with feeling.

'We've got to envision her better. Isn't that right?' I asked him. 'She'll be better soon. The surgeon does this sort of operation all the time. He said so. She'll be fine. Won't she?'

Sullivan put his hand on my shoulder and this time I didn't resent it. 'Sure, David, sure.'

For the first time in ages I felt we were on the same side. I remembered how it had been when he'd first come to St Joe's. All of us knew about his rugby career: the three caps he'd gained for Ireland in a winning team in the 1990s. He'd been my hero then. He was who I wanted to be. Even though our teams had always been successful, we became even better with Sullivan as our coach. He gave us great pep talks before games. When we were facing St Mary's, who were bigger and more powerful than us, he'd said, 'Remember, it's not how big you are, it's how big you play the game.' I'd scored a winning try for him after that. Just before a game he'd say, 'Okay, now let your game do the talking.'

This was a bigger test. I didn't care about the things that had been worrying me before Helen's accident. That was all just normal life. All I wanted was for Helen to have that too, for her to be better, to have my sister back again, always there.

And so we waited.

April Fool's Day

Midnight came. I watched the seconds tick by on the big clock on the waiting room wall and the digital calendar click to 1 April – April Fool's Day. Every year I played a joke on Helen. She'd had fizzing sugar cubes, itching powder in her clothes and plastic flies floating on the top of her coffee. If I hadn't bought anything in a joke shop, I made do with clingfilm over the loo seat, or hiding in a closet and leaping out on her. Usually she shrieked, called me a *vile toad* and wished aloud that she didn't have a younger brother. Strange, what you can miss.

We stopped talking, all of us moving about from place to place, restlessly. Someone sat, someone got up and paced around, like that game where there always has to be one of you sitting, one standing, one leaning. But this wasn't a game. It was just that no one could sleep, but no one wanted to be wide awake either because wide awake meant thinking about that surgeon working away on Helen's brain.

Finally, Mum saw the surgeon she'd spoken to coming towards us. We crowded around him.

'Helen's in the recovery room,' he told us. 'The

operation went well.'

'So she'll be alright?' Dad asked. He wanted certainty the way I had, the way I still did.

But all the surgeon would say was, 'Everything went as planned. I lifted the bone and now we have to wait. She won't be coming to for some hours.'

'Can we see her?' Mum asked.

The surgeon looked at us all. 'Just for a few minutes.'

Helen was lying still on the bed. There was a drip in her arm and tubes coming from her head, which was bandaged. By the side of the bandage I could see where some of her long blonde hair had been shaved away so the surgeon could get at her brain. She'll hate that, I thought. She was linked up to a machine that showed her heartbeat as an uneven, wavy line. Always pale, she now looked ghostly white. There were small cuts all over her face. Mum and Dad had sort of brave, unconvincing smiles on their faces, as if she could see them and they wanted to reassure her that everything was going to be alright.

Sullivan hung back, as if he didn't know whether the surgeon had included him when he said that we could see Helen for a few moments. Ian looked appalled, wide-eyed. He hated hospitals and made a fuss if he had to have so much as an injection. He hadn't spent the time I had in casualty departments to get used to them.

I knew I had to hold it together for Mum, Dad and Helen, but I wanted to punch the wall, throw a chair out of the window, or howl. It was a bit like anger, but I knew it was some different feeling I hadn't experienced before. I wanted, more than I'd ever wanted anything, for this not to be what life was like. I'd settle for any crappy thing – being relegated to the C team, any mind-numbing schoolday, treble French on an afternoon after the chips had run out in the canteen at lunchtime – anything so long as *this* wasn't happening.

'Come on,' said Dad. We trailed out and Mum and Dad tried to decide who should stay at the hospital.

'I'm staying,' said Sullivan firmly. Mum gave his arm a squeeze.

'Of course,' she said, 'but ...' she looked at Dad, '... one of us has got to take David home.'

'I'm staying too,' I said. I wanted us to stay together and all be there when Helen woke up. I was having some nightmare thoughts about how she would be changed – perhaps she would be a zombie from now on.

'You've got to see to M,' Dad reminded me. 'And you've got to get some sleep so you can take over from us. Come on, Davy.'

'We'll phone you as soon as something happens,' Mum promised.

Reluctantly, Ian agreed to go home too, so he drove us. It was hard to leave. It seemed like a betrayal. The cool of the night air hit us when we left the hospital. It was a shock that the world outside was still there, unchanged. How could everything seem so normal when our lives were so misshapen? We were quiet at first, making our way out of Dublin on the deserted roads, but then we started to talk.

'Remember last year, the night of the fire?' I asked.

'Course.'

When the houses were ablaze, Ian had rushed in to save our next-door neighbour who was deaf and had not heard the commotion until it was too late. Ian had saved her, without a thought for his precious hands. He could have been severely burnt, his music career ruined. Forget his career, he could have died.

'Did you, you know, think about dying when you were going into the fire?'

'Nah. Just did it. To tell the truth, when I thought about it afterwards, I couldn't even imagine doing it. No way!'

'But you did, Ian. You did.'

'Some things are scarier when you think about them than when you do them.' I wondered if he was thinking of what it was like to be Helen at that moment. Was she scared? Could you be scared when you were unconscious? Or was it us who were scared and Helen was just living or dying, without thought?

'Do you think she's going to get better?' I asked.

He shook his head. 'She's got to. She's got to.'

We were quiet after that. When we drove up to *The Haven* there was an unfamiliar darkness about the place. Nobody had been there to turn on the outside lights and there was none on inside either.

M started jumping up, scratching at my legs when I opened the back door and there was a puddle on the utility room floor. I mopped it up, changed his drinking water and filled the feeding bowls.

Ian went straight to his piano and started playing. Over the years, I'd developed the skill of blotting out his music, but now the sounds he started to make got through my defences. He was hammering away – I think he was playing something by Beethoven. It was frenzied, angry, like a tempest of sound. It was as if he was shouting, *No, I don't want this chaos, this pain!* Then the playing would grow softer and it sounded more like despair, *why this?* For once I didn't complain as the house shook with his playing. Ian was communicating just what I felt. I looked in on him once, but he did not see me as his hands moved along the keys like two tarantulas in deadly combat.

I wandered around the house, not quite believing that I wouldn't find Mum or Dad somewhere. I fancied hitting a few golf shots, but all the clubs were in the boot of Dad's car, still at the hospital. I found a broom and tried whacking a few rolled-up socks, but it wasn't the same. M and the kitten followed me wherever I went. They hadn't touched their food. Though both must have been hungry, they just left it. It was odd. It was as if they sensed something was wrong. I didn't go into Helen's room. Her things lying about untidily all over the place just brought back where she was and what was happening to her.

Finally, I climbed the stairs to my room. It had been a long day. M jumped onto my bed and started licking me. He licked and licked at my skin until it almost hurt, but all the time it calmed me down. Even though I was dead tired, I couldn't sleep, so I tried to watch a film while we waited, alone in the big house, M beside me and Mozart by my feet.

The piano playing had stopped. Ian had moved to the violin and was wailing on that when the house phone rang. It was Dad telling us that Helen had opened her eyes. 'So she's okay?'

He hesitated only for a split second, but it was enough for me to know that I still wasn't going to get the 100% certainty I wanted.

'She's still very groggy. The effects of the anaesthetic are only just beginning to wear off.'

'Did she recognise you?' asked Ian.

'I think she knew we were there. That's all we can expect for the moment.'

That would have to do. I climbed the stairs again and Ian didn't pick up his violin again. Finally, we slept.

Waiting, and the neighbours turn up

When I think back to the week after Helen's accident, it's a blur of jumbled, muddled days mixed with some vivid moments of fear. We forgot the date and what day of the week it was. And the time of day became important only because it affected how long it took us to get to the hospital through the traffic. We were wide awake in the middle of the night, or slumped in chairs in the hospital, completely knackered; vampires got more fresh air than we did. We were like a bunch of pandas, our eyes rimmed by dark shadows and about as slow moving. And food. No knives and forks, or plates. No meals. We ate the sort of stuff that comes wrapped in paper or polystyrene boxes. Nothing *green*, unless you count when I threw a half-eaten cheese sandwich away in the car and sat on it a few days later when it was going mouldy.

It was a week-long nightmare full of recurring monsters. But escape was coming, for although the news each day was never the 100% *she's better* that I hoped for, Helen was gradually improving. One day she smiled, the next she spoke. There were setbacks and scares, but her progress was up, not down. Like it sometimes said on my school reports, Helen was 'making progress'. She had tests done and the doctors said she was unlikely to suffer any long-term brain injury. Even the part of her head that had been shaved began to grow tufts of blonde hair.

After a week, Mum decided I should return to school. I didn't mind. I'd had the one reason for an unscheduled holiday from the place that no one would envy me for. One day, when we'd rushed to the hospital at midnight because Helen had a high temperature, I'd been drooping in the car on the way home at the time I'd normally have been heading into school. I raised my head and looked out to see some fellas in St Joe's uniform going by. And I wished I was with them.

I'd texted Abbas and Joe about what had happened, so everyone in school knew my sister had had an accident, but no one said anything to me. The wrong word and *they'd* be in intensive care.

But I suppose 'the time of Helen's accident' wasn't over until some of the old niggles returned. For example, Ian shared out the hospital visits with Mum when Dad decided to return to work, even though he was due back in London at his studies by that time. When I asked him whether he'd be in trouble for delaying going back he answered scornfully, 'I'm not a little nipper! University isn't school, Bruv.' Yup, the fake cockney was back and – Hello, normality! – Flimsy McFeeble was getting on my nerves again.

One thing did change though. Suddenly the whole neighbourhood seemed to know us. Cards and notes arrived on the doorstep. *Sorry to hear about your daughter's accident*, they'd say and be signed by people we'd never heard of. There was even one from Dimbrook Golf Club, so I guess Andrea knew what had happened. There were little gifts, too, left in the porch: cakes, pies, meals with notes saying *you'll be too busy to cook.* No longer did *The Haven* seem to be in the middle of nowhere. Range Rovers and other SUVs that I'd dodged on the winding roads now pulled into the driveway and burly farmer types in wax jackets would get out and call at the door. They were the women. Male neighbours left messages on our phone, telling us where they lived in the neighbourhood and offering lifts to the hospital, or any other help they could give. Suddenly *The Haven* was teeming with life – it had become the centre of the universe. Even little kids came round, holding home-made cards with grisly drawings of bandaged patients, or upturned cars. Some of the ones of the car were dead accurate. They even got the colour right, so I guess the site of the accident had been visited a lot before the Volkswagen was towed away.

Mum got quite tearful about it all. She couldn't wear her dressing gown all day now, even when she had been at the hospital through the night, because visitors appeared at any hour. One day it was a middle-aged man wearing a grubby vest revealing arms so tattooed they looked like Stilton cheese. His gnarled, ugly face was familiar. It was Baseball Cap. He wasn't wearing his red cap, but was holding it in his hands. Close up, he was older than I'd thought. Mike the barman hadn't told us what Baseball Cap had done to his wife, but he was the last person I'd expected to see.

'Yeah?' I asked, blocking the doorway, but Mum came to the door and invited him in. Reluctantly, I stood aside.

'Heard about youz trouble, missus,' he said.

If I didn't know better I'd have said he really was sorry for us. Mum poured him tea and gave him a full account of the accident and Helen's injuries. He nodded, muttered and mumbled, then left, without ever telling us his name. If I hadn't recognised him, we wouldn't even have known where he came from. When we opened the parcel he'd left, it was an old advertisement, in wood, the sort that goes on the wall: Guinness is Good for You.

We stared at it.

Neighbours we never knew we had would call in and if Mum were in, I'd come home to find them sitting in the kitchen with her, or touring the house. They cheered Mum up, even the batty ones, like the old lady who brought grapes and ate them all while talking about the goings-on in *The Haven* when it had been named something else and an old, faded rock star lived in it.

One day I walked in and there was Frank Lynch sitting at the kitchen table! 'Ah, here he is,' said Mum in that way that told me she had been talking about me. In the background, in the other room, Ian was playing something gloomy on the violin. 'Mr Lynch, this is David. David, Mr Lynch.'

I didn't know whether to give the dognapper a scowl, or the committee member who had my golfing fate in his hands a suck-up smile. I compromised and sent him a dazzling scowl.

'This your dog?' asked Frank Lynch. M was licking his hand.

'What?' He'd asked me that before. Trouble was, I couldn't remember what I'd answered, though I knew I hadn't admitted M was mine just in case he had been running around biting the heads off chickens. But, what the hell. Mum had probably told him anyway. 'Sure,' I said. 'He's mine.'

'You do all the walking?'

I nodded. 'All the walking.'

'It's important to walk a dog. Shouldn't have one unless you're prepared to put in the legwork.' This sounded like a pat on the back, though if he wanted my dog for himself, it could be more of a threat.

Ian came in with his violin. His eyes just flitted over Frank Lynch as if he hardly saw him. McFeeble was in serious musical mood. 'Listen. I'm going to play two versions of this piece I'm composing. Tell me which is better.'

'Hang on.' I was looking at the kitten that had followed him in. 'Who's that?'

'Who der yer fink? Mozart. He's been following me about all day.'

'No.' I checked around the place and then looked in the utility room. 'Ah yes.' I pointed through the open utility room door. 'That's Mozart.' He was lying peacefully in his shoebox.

'This ...' I pointed to the kitten looking up at us by Ian's feet, '... is not Mozart.'

Mum, Ian and Frank Lynch stared at the two sleeping kittens. To an idle observer, they probably looked like twins, both long-haired tabbies, but I'd got to know Mozart's markings well. He had a large white patch on his throat and stripes like a tiger along his nose. This new kitten had a smaller patch of white on its throat, no stripes but white back paws that looked like sports socks.

'We're plagued by feral cats around this time of year,' said Frank Lynch.

'Oh, Mozart's brought his little brother in!' Mum scooped him up. M tried bouncing up to see what she was holding. I lifted him up so he could see. He did not growl, having got used to the sight and smell of kitten.

Mum stroked the new kitten. 'David, get some milk,' she whispered.

'Why are you whispering?' I asked loudly. This kitten's reaction to strangers was not to hiss and bare its sharp little teeth as Mozart's had been. Perhaps, if he and Mozart were from the same litter, he thought this was his natural home. He widened his green eyes and stared at us.

'Ah, it's so gentle. It must be female,' said Mum.

'In what universe?' I asked as I put down a saucer of milk. Frank Lynch smiled.

Mum was fussing over the new kitten. 'Can I name this one?' I asked. No way was it going to be thrown out. Mozart greeted the new arrival as if he recognised him. They went together like Ant and Dec. Mum nodded.

'I'm still waiting,' yelled Ian. When we had turned to

look at him, he repeated, 'Listen to these two versions of this piece I'm composing and tell me which is better.' He played a frenzied, jangling, discordant piece of music, worse than bagpipes, the sort of music that used to make great-uncle Albert turn his cap back to front and complain that he had a stomach-ache. Finally, mercifully, it stopped.

'Okay,' I said,' I prefer the second.'

'I haven't played the second yet.'

'Yeah, but it can't be worse than the first. *Therefore*, I prefer it.'

'Philistine!'

I started to say something that Mum would give out to me for when I reminded myself that the esteemed committee member was present. The etiquette of golf had to be respected.

Frank Lynch broke the silence. 'Anyhow, as I told your mother, the club committee is meeting next Monday.'

'You mean ...?'

'They will decide about your membership.' Now I knew why I'd been the subject of conversation. Mum had been talking me up so that Frank Lynch recommended me to the committee. I suspected that all this recommendation stuff was a smoke-screen. It was Frank Lynch who would decide whether I got into Dimbrook or not, Frank Lynch who would launch my brilliant golfing career, or sink it. I offered him a biscuit.

Third nutty neighbour

Sometimes I visited Helen after school, taking the bus across the city and then waiting for a lift home with Mum or Dad – whoever was on hospital duty. The first time I went, Sullivan turned up too. He was back working at school, but he'd handed the rugby training over to McCaffrey – I presume so he would have more time to visit Helen. When I saw him in the hospital he was carrying a huge bunch of red roses, so his ferocious bullet head loomed out of a forest of flowers. He brought Helen gifts everyday, 'cute' cuddly toys as well as flowers. I don't get how they're meant to make ill people feel better. Now, if they'd let me bring in M and the kittens: that was a show! The whole hospital would be entertained by what they got up to. I'd named the second kitten Tiger, after Tiger Woods, of course. I was dead set on it not being another musician. Ian had objected. 'I fink Trigger's a stoopid name for a little cat.'

'*Tiger*, not Trigger.' He was getting it wrong just to wind me up. It was working. 'I suppose you'd want to call him Beethoven.'

'Nice one, 'e was deaf! That would be right for that dawg of yours. Judging by the way that mutt ignores commands,

I fink 'e could be.'

'He's a *pedigree*. We've got papers proving it. He's not going to obey every stupid order he's given. That's what was wrong with the Nazis.'

'Who are you calling a Nazi?'

'For pity's sake, give it a rest you two,' Mum said wearily.

Now M had two balls of fur to tussle with. They were his pack. No way would they be treated separately. Even if I put down three bowls – two with kitten food, one with dog food – the kittens would wait for M to have his fill, then scramble to what was left, their heads touching as they tucked in. By now, M usually went for the kitten food and left them the dog food. He was their overlord because he was bigger, stronger and fiercer. Yet he groomed them, licking their ears until they were wet and sleek.

I was telling Helen all this when Sullivan arrived. Mum rushed forward and hugged him. The accident had brought on a hugging habit – possibly an addiction. If this went on, she'd have to join *Huggers Anonymous*. 'Hello, my name is Elizabeth Stirling and I'm a huggaholic.' I was back to a strict No Hugging policy. There's a sign I'd seen in a Dublin shop: Please do not ask for credit as a refusal often offends. I want my own: Please do not ask for a hug as a refusal often offends. P.S. ditto air-kissing. No way was I going to get that close to Sullivan, though since the night of the accident we'd been friendly enough. He had showed he cared, I'll give him that.

Helen's face was still a mess and she seemed more worried about this than about her other injuries, even her broken ankle. She was fussing, too, about the way her hair was long one side and short the other. She had even darker circles around her eyes than we had. It reminded me of how I'd looked when my nose was broken the rugby season before last, though her nose still looked straight. She had six or seven cuts on her forehead and around one eye, but they weren't deep. Mum spent a lot of time reassuring her she wouldn't have any scars. Helen had got her mitts on a hand mirror, and all the time I was telling her about M and the kittens, she was holding it up to her face.

'Are you *sure* this won't leave a mark? How about this one?' she kept asking. She was especially worried about a two-inch gash from her eye to her hairline. By age twelve, I'd had dozens like that.

When Sullivan and the red roses appeared, Mum and I 'tactfully' went off to the canteen.

'All these cuts will heal,' Mum assured Helen when we got back to her and she was *still* going on about her face. Someone had sent a box of fudge and Mum was steadily eating her way through the lot. 'Davy has bigger cuts on his knees virtually every week.'

True, but then nobody, as far as I knew, thought I had beautiful knees. In Classics last year we'd learnt how a woman called Helen had started the Trojan War – because she was so beautiful! One of the Trojan princes took her back to his city, which annoyed her Greek husband. So all the Greeks attacked Troy, besieging it for ten years. Helen's face *launched a thousand ships*.

My sister hadn't launched any ships, but her face and

figure had sunk a few eejits. Having lugged Helen of Troy off, I bet that prince regretted it. She'd be in Troy, battles going on all around her, heads being lopped off, cries of anguish from every quarter, and she'd be there with her mirror going, '*Am I getting any wrinkles? Does my bum look big in this?*'

The Monday after Frank Lynch came round, I took the earliest bus I could home from school. The next day I was going to be back training with the B team and I wanted some good news on the golfing front to compensate. The Dimbrook committee could be meeting to discuss my application right now.

I called in at the village shop on the way home, buying some crisps and chocolate. The shopkeeper served me without a word. I went outside the shop, then back in again. 'That sign above your shop ...' I started.

He raised an eyebrow. 'Yes?' He didn't exactly strike me as a 'the customer is always right' sort of fella.

'It says *McDonnell's 24/7.*'

'That's correct.'

'So, Mr McDonnell, what's with the *24/7*?'

'My name isn't McDonnell.'

'It isn't? So why have you called the shop *McDonnell's*? Oh, I get it! I bet the fella who owned the shop before you was called McDonnell. Right?'

'*Wrong.*' You could see he was getting a whole heap of satisfaction out of saying that. 'The fella before the fella who last owned the shop was called McDonnell. If we change the name, our customers will be confused.'

'I think that ship's already sailed!' So, finally, I could get back to my point. 'And what's with the 24/7?'

He raised his eyebrow even higher. 'Yes?'

'That means twenty-four hours, seven days. You should be open *all the time*.'

'I've been here years. You think I haven't been open twenty-four hours?'

'Yes, but twenty-four hours *one after another* – 24/7 means *all the time*!'

'Oh, so you think I shouldn't sleep, is that it? What am I meant to do – wait here in the hope that you're going to spend two euro?'

I went out, shaking my head. He probably had a berth on Nutters Lane!

Back home, I waited for the phone call. The phone never stopped ringing, but it was never Dimbrook or Frank Lynch. More waiting.

I had started practicing again, sometimes just going into the grounds of *The Haven* and hitting a few balls there. The grass was tougher than a golf course, but that was good practice for getting into the 'rough'. I reckon if you can handle the difficult conditions, you're a winner. The winds that swirl around the place also tested the accuracy of my shots and I had the pond in the bottom field for a water hazard. The only thing missing was a sand bunker. I planned to convince Dad to let me build one instead of a rockery. At least it would be useful. What's a rockery, after all? Just a heap of small rocks. Ireland's full of heaps of rocks.

After dark, I'd go to the range, walking past the very spot where we had found Helen's car. The range had flood-lights. Now that we were known in the area, I'd get the culchie nod and questions about Helen from the other golfers. They saw my swing and were impressed. I was creaming it. The sooner I got on a proper golf course, the better. Tiger Woods was playing when he was three, so I'd already lost ten years – the same number those Trojans wasted fighting over Helen.

I heard about the competition, too. Everybody who belonged to Dimbrook was agreed that they needed juve-nile members. Time and time again they'd say there was only one talented young player: the famous Andy Donald-son. I didn't react when they mentioned their 'star', just noted the details, like marking out the biggest, toughest player in the opposing team. The one to beat.

'There's only Andy playing off single figures,' one old fella told me. I tried to look unimpressed, but a single figure handicap was some opposition. I practiced more.

At rugby training the following day, even though I'd lived on junk food for two weeks and was dead tired, I dis-covered that my body wanted the workout. I'd jogged around the pitch before the stragglers in the B team had tied their shoelaces. I was twice round and lapping some of them again. Then when we got down to practice moves, I tackled more rapidly and more vigorously than any of them. When I'd first been relegated, they'd singled me out for booting and winding. Only Abbas acted as if I was on the same side, but now they backed off. The thing is, if they think you're unbeatable, you *are* unbeatable. It's true what Sullivan says: all sports are games of the mind. I pulverised them.

Then home, and to golf. I was planning to have a bath before I set out for the range. The bath water was running and I was just peeling my trousers away from my knees – mud and blood had glued them together – when I heard a splash. I rushed into the bathroom, or tried to: with my trousers around my knees, I didn't get as far as the doorway before I fell over. I struggled up and ran. One of the kittens was thrashing about in the water, its mouth gaping as it struggled to keep afloat. I hauled it out, grabbed a garment off the towel rail and wrapped it around the tiny drenched body. As I held it, I felt the pounding of its heart. It must have been terrified. Cats hate water. M bounded up the stairs, as if he knew one of his pack was in trouble. He leapt up onto the bed where I was using the jacket as a towel and took over the drying. As the fur dried and the markings became clearer, I recognised Tiger. I'd saved Tiger from drowning. That seemed like a good omen for my golfing future.

Welcome Home

'Look at that view. Dad, look at that–'
'I'm driving, Davy.'

'Mum, look at that view. You won't get a view like that in Dublin.'

'It *is* Dublin, you cretin!' said Ian, safely out of my reach with Mum in the back seat. It was Saturday morning and they were going to visit Helen. I was ready to play rugby. I was still on the B team and there had been no news from Dimbrook or Frank Lynch, but I was coming round to seeing the advantages of living in the wilderness.

I wound down the window. 'Smell that fresh air! That's the mountains …'

'Whata you doin'? Planning a career with the tourist board?' asked Ian. 'And close that winder. It's freezing back 'ere.'

When we got closer to Dublin, I pointed out the litter, the traffic and how people on the streets were too busy to give the culchie nod. Silence.

I had a new plan of action. My problem list had changed: now I wanted to make sure that we stayed living at *The Haven*. Helen's complaints about having to drive once again between Dublin and Kildare were threatening to uproot us all, and just when I had begun to see country life in a new light. There were benefits, advantages, certain attractions that I just wouldn't have in Dublin: the golf club nearby, the fresh air, the space for M and the kittens to play, my attic room and Andrea. The list wasn't necessarily in that order! Of course, the moment I decided I was actually happy was the moment my parents decided maybe another move would be a good idea. I just couldn't win: when I complained, they told me to get used to it; when I got used to it, they started to complain. I wasn't going to give up without a fight, though. No way. At every opportunity I reminded them of all the reasons they moved to the sticks in the first place. And I would continue to do so until they saw sense.

Rugby was at the opposing side's school. Dad dropped me off and I went into the changing rooms, charging myself up for the game ahead. The school was nearly as strong at rugby as St Joe's, but when their B team lined up, I almost laughed aloud. 'Okay, we can take them,' I assured our captain. They looked like a bunch of invalids, knock-kneed, pale-faced, not fit enough for ten-pin bowling, let alone rugby. I could have selected a stronger team from the patients on Helen's ward at the hospital.

The game started. We took the ball and – give a few minutes here and there – we kept it. We ran, weaving in and out like we'd been trained to do, while they stood like statues, as if waiting for some signal to start that never came. Whether they were tired, mesmerised, or just out-classed, I don't know. I was too busy scoring tries to work it out. We hit touch so often, we lost track of the score. Finally it ended, with the score a very satisfying 52 to 3. That was one of the biggest wins we'd ever had and it was made all the sweeter when we heard that our A team had lost to them 9 to 14. Cahill hadn't scored a single try.

After showering and changing, I set off for the hospital, where I was going to get a lift home with Mum and Dad. When I got there, they were celebrating the fact that Helen had been told she was ready to go home. She looked a lot better. The cuts on her face were healing up and she'd had a hairdresser friend visit her to give her a short, trendy haircut, so she no longer looked like a freak. She was sounding more like her old self, too.

'I think Helen's developed a phobia about driving. She says she dreads the thought of getting behind the wheel again,' Mum said.

'It's the rest of us who should have a phobia about that,' I muttered. Everyone but me seemed to have forgotten that we knew before the accident that Helen was a bad driver.

'It's that road, it's so winding. It's not safe,' Helen complained.

'Yeah, but you knew it had bends in it when you were driving on it. They didn't just appear, did they?'

'That's enough, David,' said Mum.

'Okay, bendy roads.' I slapped my wrist. 'Naughty bendy roads …'

Helen was going to be discharged the next day. She wanted Sullivan to collect her, so as we drove home Mum talked about having a little home-coming celebration.

'At least we've got to know our neighbours because of all this,' Dad said. 'Now we have some people to invite,' which was true.

'It's really important to have good neighbours, isn't it?' I said. 'In Dublin everyone is so busy, too busy to care, but we're lucky having neighbours who take the time and are considerate. Don't you think?' Mum and Dad exchanged a look and said nothing. I may have to modify the plan of action!

The next day a prolonged, plaintive, high-pitched cry of pain woke me. It was blood-chilling. It was Ian playing the violin. Mozart and Tiger leapt from the bed and started scratching furiously. I think Ian can reach notes only animals can hear because they go frantic when he's playing. The wailing went on.

'Shut up!' I shouted. 'Shut up!' But the damage had been done. I was awake, on my only day of rest. My muscles were aching, but I remembered it was because I had shouldered my way to the touchline again and again in the game the day before, so I didn't care. What a scoreline: 52 to 3! When the headmaster announced the teams' results on Monday, that would sound a hell of a lot better than the A team's lousy 9 to 14. I slid down the banisters to breakfast; there were smells of cooking coming from the kitchen.

Mum was mixing chocolate cake mixture and talking on the phone, her head on one side. Obviously, she was informing the whole universe about Helen. She was saying, 'Yes, she's had a terrible time of it lately.' She'd been saying this to everyone. I wondered whether, when I ran my first car into a ditch, it would count as *having a terrible time*.

A whole bunch of people were being invited to welcome Helen home. It was going to be the first time *The Haven* had been full. Ian was composing a special piece of music to mark the occasion. I reckoned I'd stay for ten minutes, then make my getaway. I had M to walk and golf to practice. Hell, if they all stayed too long, I might even go and do some homework!

By midday, Dad was arranging drinks and glasses on the sideboard in the dining room and Mum was wearing her party gear: don't ask! Bang on time, the neighbourhood arrived. I guess they've never heard of being politely late. The farmers were in their idea of 'best' clothes – thick tweeds and polished brogues, their wind-battered complexions making them look flushed and strangely excited. There were fellas in suits who travelled into Dublin during the week together with their wives who had disturbingly loud, braying voices. Baseball Cap turned up and stood by the makeshift bar, eating peanuts. Then, sailing up in their convertibles and garishly coloured vehicles, the Beautiful People arrived. With their fake tans, fiercely styled hair

and long, pointy nails, they began air-kissing and shriek-
ing *Darling!* at one other. It was *The Invasion of the Body
Snatchers*. The neighbours looked on, appalled. I beat a
retreat after a fella with a ponytail threw his hands in the
air and cried out, 'So this is little Davy!' Who did he
expect to meet in the Stirling home – Lawrence of Arabia?

The kitchen was full of food, the chocolate cake deco-
rated with *Welcome Home Helen* and Mum was about to
pick it up and carry it through to take pride of place on the
dining-room table, when I heard Ian hissing at me from
the doorway. He gets dead furtive when there are guests in
the house.

'Davy. Get out 'ere. I want a word wiv you!'

'Me?' I was standing by the kitchen sink, licking out the
remains of the chocolate cake mixture.

'Wot's the idea?'

'What idea do you mean – the idea of gravity? Evolu-
tion? Baked bean pizza?'

'Wot do yer fink you're playing at?' He came into the
kitchen, holding up a jacket. 'What did you do to this?'

I shrugged. 'Nothing. You don't think, sorry, you don't
fink I'd wear anything of yours, do you? I've got more taste.'
Then I recognised the crumpled jacket he was holding up
like it was exhibit A. It was what I'd grabbed when I'd
fished the kitten out of the bath. 'Hang on, Ian. It was an
emergency. I–'

'Oh right, now comes the great excuse to explain why
you're not to blame, why you're not in the wrong. Because
you couldn't be, could you? No, you're *baby David*. Never

put a foot wrong. Butter wouldn't melt … That was *my* jacket and you had no right.'

That was it! I grabbed the jacket and threw it to the floor, then went for him. I held him in a headlock as he waved his arms about and squealed like a piglet. We knocked against the furniture. The back door opened and Sullivan stood there, with a figure in shadow behind him. The smile disappeared from his face as Helen's *Welcome Home* cake crashed to the floor.

Oops!

Mum didn't help by leaning backwards against the kitchen units, her hands gripping the top and a convincing look of horror on her face – as if we'd been about to set upon *her*. When the cake crashed down, she rushed towards it, but Ian and I froze for a second, me staring at Sullivan and Ian craning his neck to give Sullivan a ghastly smile. Finally, I let go of Ian's neck.

'Hello.' Sullivan's eyes were cold as he looked at Ian and me. 'I came in to make sure there was somewhere Helen could rest,' he went on, giving me a murderous look, as if he thought I'd been planning to beat her up, too. I remembered the question he'd asked me in History class, the one that resulted in my '*Why I must concentrate*' essay: can you give examples of violence being counterproductive? I was sure my headlocking Ian wasn't going to do me any favours.

We had an audience by this time. Hearing the noise, some of the guests had trundled through. Some were staring at Sullivan, some at the debris of cake. Then the figure behind him came into view. It was Andrea. She bent down to help Mum, who was scooping lumps of chocolate cake onto a plate.

'Let me help you with that, Mrs Stirling.'

Sullivan started to help too, and some of the guests joined in.

Ian and I both got the hint and bent down to help as well, which meant there was a crowd of us scrambling to pick up a few crumbs, crumbs which M, Mozart and Tiger were hoovering up the straightforward way – by eating them.

Finally, Sullivan stood up. ' Helen's waiting in the car.' Some of the Beautiful People whooped with delight, but to me the words sounded like an accusation. They followed Sullivan back out to the car. Ian, scowling, muttered, 'I'm gonna play her in.' I was left with Mum and Andrea.

Shock news about Tiger

I was looking anywhere but at Andrea. Mum had her *I have survived an ordeal* face on, but she began to chat away. I knew what she was doing – letting me know that, although she carried the heavy burden of sons who were out of control, she, at least, knew how to behave. She laid on the charm with a trowel, sounding even more English than usual.

'How *nice* of you to come to our little party. You're *a friend of David's*, aren't you? We've been so worried that he's *lonely* since we moved here.'

'Helen's waiting in the car,' I reminded her. I didn't know what I was going to say to Andrea, but I sure didn't want Mum painting a picture of me as some pathetic baby.

'Oh! Do excuse me.' She gave me a *how can you do this to me?* expression before leaving. I knew I'd get her *brawling like a couple of hooligans* lecture when she got me on my own.

There was silence, broken only by M greeting Andrea and the kittens jumping on the table to get a closer look at her. From outside came the sound of Ian's frenetic fiddling.

'Want to come through?' I asked. It was meant to sound hospitable, but came out sulky. Andrea nodded, following me through to the sitting room. At the same time,

Sullivan came through the French windows with Helen in his arms, the Beautiful People all around, like some sort of bizarre procession. One ankle was in plaster with her foot and painted toenails sticking out. For once, she wasn't wearing high heels. Sullivan had to twist to manoeuvre around the furniture and I could tell he was doing it with extra force because he was annoyed. I got out of the way, but tried to look as if I was ready to assist, hoping *helpful brotherly manner* would counterbalance the *prone to violent outbursts* impression.

Helen had her arms around Sullivan's neck and when he put her down on the sofa, she kept them there for a while. Beautiful People tapped their hearts as if to say *how romantic*, but this is not how you want to see your rugby coach! I realised that during Helen's convalescence he would be around a lot. It would be like being under constant surveillance, my own CCTV following me around.

Ian put his violin on the piano and announced, 'This is in honour of your return. I've composed it specially.' The Cockney had gone *down the Swanney* again.

Crash went his hands on the keys, followed by frenzy, his fingers tumbling over each other. It was like a nervous breakdown translated into sounds. It went on for ages, long enough for me to decide that the next time I was in hospital, my special request would be that he celebrated my return with a deep, abiding hush. But the others seemed to like it, Mum and Dad smiling proudly and Andrea looking as if she was really listening. When he'd finished, there was applause. The guests seemed to be getting into the party spirit, some of the locals even managing to speak to the Beautiful People.

Then Dad made a speech – as if our eardrums hadn't suffered enough. It was along the lines of, *Thank you all for coming. Appreciate sympathy and support at this difficult time. Much loved daughter. Not her fault she's a lousy driver* – no, just kidding about the last bit. Not that I was listening. Andrea was standing by my side and I was hoping against hope that the Stirlings wouldn't show me up any further.

Dad got his round of applause, then said cheerfully, 'Bring in the cake!'

Mum said hurriedly, 'Food is set out in the dining room, everyone.' Then, with a look to me that meant *You owe me, big time*, she added, 'David, perhaps you could show our guests the way.' There was no perhaps about it. I led them through, gave them plates and cutlery and generally did a good impression of a waiter. I was hoping that Andrea wouldn't leave, but every chance I got to check, she was chatting to Helen. Baseball Cap was still lurking in a corner, shovelling food in as if he hadn't eaten for a month.

Finally, I was free to get back to Andrea. She was laughing at something Helen had said. She looked up when she saw me and said, 'I've got some news for you. Your application to join Dimbrook – it's been accepted.'

'Yes!' I'd have punched the air if she hadn't seen me punching my brother earlier. It was the news I'd been waiting for. Now there was a point to all the practicing I was doing. Soon, I'd get out on a real golf course. 'Thanks,' I said.

'Yes, well done,' said Sullivan, sourly.

'Excellent news,' enthused Dad.

I was hoping that gave me an excuse to leave the party, so I said to Andrea, 'Do you want to come to the range?'

'Can't, thanks, but I'll see you at the club sometime.'

'Show your friend out,' ordered Mum. That's the trouble with having guests, it induces chronic instruction-giving in parents. It's all part of their attempt to prove to the outside world that they're bringing you up properly. By now I was ready for a bit of parental neglect.

I led Andrea out through the kitchen. The kittens were on the work surface, enjoying the remains of a raspberry pavlova.

Andrea picked one up. 'Aren't they cute? What's his name?'

'That's Mozart.' I picked up the other one, feeling that the conversation had taken a turn for the better. 'And this is Tiger.'

'Hello, Tiger,' she said as she picked up the kitten and pressed him against her cheek.

'I named him after Tiger Woods,' I explained. Free of parental scrutiny, I just couldn't stop. 'Four times Open champion. He wasn't winning until he reworked his swing. It's flatter and wider.' She did play golf after all, so she should be able to follow. 'The intention was to produce a longer, more consistent path through the hitting zone. It didn't work at first. His start to the season was shaky, to say the least. Then, at Augusta, it all came together. The low point was a putt for eagle that rolled off

the thirteenth green …' I stopped. She looked a bit per-
plexed. I thought she was going to ask a question.

'Sure, but …'

'What?'

'Tiger Woods is a man. This …' she held the kitten up,
'… is a female. But you knew that, right?'

I cursed quietly. Mum had actually been right! I grabbed
Mozart and turned him upside-down. I was relieved to see
that he was certainly male. Well, at least there were female
tigers. It was the slight smile on Andrea's face I wasn't so
happy about, like I didn't know the difference between
male and female. If ever there was a time to change the
subject, it was now.

'So … you and Frank Lynch related then?' It seemed a
safe bet. She'd been at his bungalow when I'd walked by
with Joe and Abbas and here she was, bringing messages
from him.

'Yes, he's my granddad.'

Andrea Lynch. 'I should thank him,' I said, ' for recommending me to the committee.'

'Tell you what. Why don't you call in now? I've got to
get home, but Gramps might have time to show you round
the course.'

'Yeah.' I liked that suggestion. I went to the utility room
and hoisted my golf clubs over my shoulder.

'You won't need those,' Andrea said. 'He might be able
to show you round, but the course'll be packed on a
Sunday afternoon.'

Disappointed, I set the golf clubs down.

'Why don't you bring your dog?' she asked. 'They're allowed on the course so long as they're on leads.'

If she wasn't the best-looking girl I'd ever seen, I would have asked, 'So, what is it with your family and pedigree dogs?'

I wasn't going to let M out of my sight. At least this way he'd get his walk and I'd have an expert show me the golf course. Course knowledge is very important in the game of golf. So I agreed and Andrea and I walked over the fields to Nutters Lane. 'Gramps' was in. I thanked him for recommending me to the committee and he agreed to show me round the course. We walked for over two miles, with Frank Lynch giving me a comprehensive guide to each hole. By the time we'd finished, I knew the par for each hole, the water hazards and the bunkers. I was so ready to play.

When I thanked him he said, 'So, when do you want to play a round?'

'As soon as possible!'

He thought. 'How about Saturday morning?'

I shook my head. 'I play rugby then. I don't get back till after two.'

'Right. It will have to be Saturday afternoon. It'll be crowded, mind. Think you can handle it?'

'Sure!'

'Then Saturday afternoon it is. I'll phone with a tee time.'

'Great! Thanks!'

I went home to get some food and my golf clubs. There

were still some of Helen's friends on the premises, but loads of food left because they're on diets the whole time. I resolved to practice everyday before Saturday.

Down at the range, the bays were full. I had to wait behind some man in green tartan golfing trousers. He was no beginner and his chipping was accurate, but when he was driving, he couldn't get a ball as far as the one hundred-and-fifty-yard marker. When I moved into the bay, he leaned back and watched me the way I had watched him.

After I had sent a dozen balls flying past the two hundred-yard marker, he said, 'Start young. You youngsters are lucky! I didn't get a chance to play until I was in my forties. You a member at Dimbrook? Haven't seen you there.'

'I've just got in.'

'You mean you're new to this game?'

I nodded. He made a whistling noise through his teeth. 'Nice one. Andy Donaldson is a great little player, considering, but you've got the potential to be first class. Well, keep up the good work.'

I nodded my thanks as he pulled his bag away. I went on practicing, looking forward to the day when I knocked Andy Donaldson off his perch.

Minty

It soon seemed as if Helen had always been on that sofa. If I lay on it for more than an hour or two, Dad sarcastically referred to me as *a permanent fixture* and Mum asked if I'd lost the power in my legs, but now Helen took over the whole room. She lay there, grimacing with pain when anyone looked in her direction, surrounded by magazines, foul-smelling nail polish and other make-up, surfing through the TV channels, looking for some junk about *relationships*.

At night, I had to carry her up the stairs. She moaned the entire way. 'Be careful. Watch out for my ankle. It hurts, you know.' I did know because she was telling us the whole time. I cracked a rib once during rugby practice and that was painful enough, so of course I realised that a cracked skull and broken ankle weren't fun, but then neither was my sister. The more we did for her, the more she acted the invalid; Mum might as well have put on a nurse's uniform! But what really got me was that Helen talked as if some great injustice had left her like this, not her own crummy driving.

'Surely she's meant to be *exercising* by now,' I said to Mum.

'When the doctor says so.'

'Is she going for a check-up soon?'

'Next week. I'll have to drive her in. That's the disadvantage of living so far out, everything involves a journey.'

'But I do that journey six days a week and it doesn't bother me!'

'Well, we can't all be like you, David.'

Mum was still a little off with me since the cake incident. I guess having to watch Helen turning herself into a moaning, spoilt brat was penance for putting Ian in a headlock. I hadn't been punished, though Dad had shouted like crazy when Mum told him, turning it into a scene in vivid technicolor. I got the usual lecture about being irresponsible, likely to end up in Mountjoy prison if I didn't learn to control my temper, and sending my mother to an early grave. All this because *I rescued a cat from drowning*.

Anyway, I wasn't bothered about all that because my first round of golf was coming up. Frank Lynch had phoned to say my starting time, the *tee time*, was 2.30pm on Saturday. That meant I'd have to be straight off the bus after rugby, back home to collect my clubs and then onto the course, no time to spare.

I practiced my putting and chipping every evening, some days going up to the range. When I was home earlier and it was still light, I'd go into the grounds and practice there, saving the €6 it cost at the range.

Saturday came with rain and wind. At rugby, we trounced the opposition again. They didn't see us coming.

I scored four tries – *bam, bam, bam, bam* – one after another. I'd showered, changed and was tying my shoelaces with five minutes to catch the bus when Frazier led in the A team. They trailed by quietly, heads down, feet dragging on the concrete floor, so I knew they were a bunch of losers. No need to ask whether they'd won or not. But I asked anyway.

'How did you lot get on?'

There was no answer from Frazier and his cronies, but a few of the team mumbled something.

I pushed on. 'What? What was the score?'

'Thirty-seven to six.'

'Thirty-seven to six? *Thirty-seven* to … *six!* Frazier here can't even count as far as thirty-seven.' While Frazier glowered, the rest of the B team echoed my disgust. We had our victory to make us superior.

'What went wrong? Were you asleep? Cahill, did you score?' I asked my replacement. He didn't answer, just skulked away. 'I'll take that as a *no!*' I shouted after him. I hoped McCaffrey could work out what the A team was missing: *me*.

I was feeling great, until I realised the time. I ran to the bus stop, but I was too late. I'd missed the bus. The next one would get me into Ballykreig at 2.30pm – precisely my tee time. Even if I played in the clothes I wore, my golf clubs were at *The Haven*. There wouldn't be time for food either, and I'd burnt up a lot of energy on the rugby field. I spent all the money I had buying burgers and chips and ate them as I waited, cursing, for the next bus.

It came on time. If it had been late, I'd have had no chance of making my tee time. Lolling onboard, still cursing, as the bus chugged along, I realised that its route took it past Dimbrook before it arrived in the village. If I could get someone from home to bring my golf clubs to the course and I got off there, I might just make it. Trouble was, there was no bus stop at the club and I did not rate my chances of persuading the grim-looking driver to make an unscheduled stop. I would have to jump off as the bus turned the sharp bend just after the club. If I threw my bag off first, then threw myself off after it, I should roll gently into the soft ditch. It was that or miss my first round of golf. No way! I was going to make a leap for it.

I phoned home. Ian answered. He wasn't first in line of those eager to do me a favour, but he was going to be a lot less upset at the sight of me jumping from a moving bus than Mum or Dad.

'You busy?' I asked, in my friendliest manner.

'Wot der yer want?' he asked suspiciously.

'I didn't tell you how much I enjoyed that bit of music you wrote for Helen,' I told him. That was honest enough. How much had I enjoyed it? Not one bit. Had I told him? No.

'Wot're you after?'

'Look, can you just bring my golf clubs to Dimbrook? It won't take you more than ten minutes.'

'Get 'em yourself.'

'I can't. I'll miss my tee time.'

'Your tea time? Why should I care about your stomach?'

I kept my patience. '*Tee* time, nothing to do with … look, you've got to help me out or I'll be *minty*.'

'Wot?'

'You know, *After Eight* mints, after eight – late.' I'd given him a bit of cockney rhyming slang he didn't know. I could sense he'd weakened.

'Right! Don't want a bruvver of mine to be minty … wot's in it for me?'

'I'll owe you one.' I cursed again at the thought of how he'd milk that, but I wasn't going to give up.

'You'll owe me big time. Right? *Right?*'

'Right.'

The obvious had occurred to him. ''Ere, there's no bus stop by Dimbrook. 'Ow are you gonna …'

'Can't hear you. My … battery's … low …' I clicked the phone off. My plan was in place.

A mile or so before Dimbrook, I made my way to the front of the bus. I was going to engage the driver in conversation if I could. I reckoned he'd go slower if he was talking: he looked like the sort of fella who couldn't walk and chew gum at the same time. I'd thought of a question that would throw him, even though in the process I'd look like a moron.

'Does this bus go to Dublin?' I asked.

He stepped on the brakes and stared at me. 'This place look like Dublin to you, boyoo?' he asked. We passed the entrance to Dimbrook. Ian was standing by the gates, my golf clubs by his side. The crucial bend wasn't far away.

'Guess not,' I said, trying to keep my voice level. 'Could you …'

Then I yanked the door open and flung my bag. The driver yelled something, but I was out! I jumped for the ditch, hit the bank and rolled. The ditch wasn't as soft as I thought it was going to be. I rolled over some sort of plant that tore my jacket and cut into my arm. When I hit the bottom of the ditch, I felt chilly water soaking my skin. I cursed the rain, stood up and brushed myself down. No injuries, except a sore shoulder and a scratch along my face. I had no time to waste. I retrieved my bag and ran towards Dimbrook.

Ian stared at me when I reached him. 'Did you …? Did I see …?' he started, but I hadn't time to waste.

'Yup,' I said, taking my clubs. 'Thanks for these.' I tried to steady my breathing as I ran towards the Starter's Office. I didn't even have time to check my watch.

Frank Lynch was waiting at the Office. He was wearing yellow waterproofs, which made him look like a fisherman. Me, I guess I looked more like something pulled out of the sea. The rain was bouncing off Frank and seeping into me.

'You playing like that?' he shouted in the wind. 'You're soaked through.'

No kidding! 'Just a bit damp,' I said, pulling off my

jacket and squeezing the water out of it.

'And you're bleeding!'

'Rugby injury,' I explained. 'You should see the other fella.'

Nothing was going to spoil this moment. I was on a *real* golf course. This was the beginning, a day to remember. I was going to play with a veteran, someone who knew this particular course like the back of his hand.

We signed in precisely on time, with not a second to spare, and approached the first tee. Some members were sitting in the bar, looking warm and cosy and staring out of the large window that gave a perfect view of the first tee. Frank Lynch teed up and hit a shot clean and straight.

I took my driver and hit the ball. It sailed high and landed 170 yards up the fairway, a bit further than Frank's. What with the wind and rain, I knew that wasn't bad. He said nothing, just grabbed his golf trolley and headed towards the balls. I followed him, carrying my golf bag over my shoulder. The rain was pouring down my face, but I didn't mind. Chipping proved difficult in the conditions, but all my putting practice paid off and I was scoring mainly sixes and sevens. Frank was doing the same. Judging from his technique, I guessed he'd been a first-class golfer when he was younger, but he no longer had the strength to drive powerfully, though he was still accurate in his putting. I knew that I could learn a lot from him.

On the fourteenth hole I made *par*, which means I did

nearly as well as a professional. I averaged par plus two, which is a *double bogey* to those of us who know the lingo, and ended with a score of 109. Frank scored 106. I'd lost, but I'd lost to an old fella who'd been playing golf for sixty years, and most of it at Dimbrook, so I wasn't too cut up about it. I'd made a few mistakes, like slicing the ball or over-hitting a few putts, but they were faults I knew I could correct. I wouldn't lose to Frank Lynch second time.

As we returned to the clubhouse, the wind propelling us along, we met two men who greeted him.

'This young lad's just scored 109 on his first round!' Frank said, making it sound like a boast.

'Well done!' they both said. One of them added, 'Good, the club needs some fresh talent.' My 109 was starting to seem better than okay to me.

I thanked Frank Lynch and made my way home. It had stopped raining and the skies had cleared. I was actually starting to dry off as I made my way towards home, my clubs over one shoulder and my school bag in the other. I saw Andrea walking along the lane towards me.

'How did you get on?' she asked. She had known what time Frank and I were playing and I wondered whether she had been waiting to see me when I'd finished. I liked the thought of that.

'I can drive the ball two hundred yards!' I boasted
'Nice one!'
She sounded dead impressed.
'I scored 109, but I'll do better next time.' She nodded.
'Then I want to play this *star* they've got up at the club.'

Something must have made me crazy. I even did that speechmarks thing with my hands as I said *star*, like Helen does sometimes.

'Star?' she said. 'Who's that?'

'His name's Andy Donaldson, and one day soon I'm going to whip his ass!'

Exit, Flimsy McFeeble; Enter, Another Genius

'**S**o what exactly are your opening hours?' Flimsy McFeeble and I were in the village shop. My brother had confirmed that 24/7 meant twenty-four hours of seven days in the week. In other words, *all the time*. Even in Ballykrieg it meant *all the time*. It meant *all the time* all the time, basically.

'You mean on Tuesdays?' replied the shopkeeper.

'What? No, not on Tuesdays.' This was exasperating, like we were in a parallel universe. It was Sunday and he was open, though the Sunday before the shop had been closed. 'Everyday. We mean, what are your opening hours *everyday*?' I explained.

'Depends. Now Tuesdays ...' Ian groaned.

'Never mind. Thanks.' I handed him the money and McFeeble and I left, laughing as soon as we were out of earshot.

Ian whistled through his teeth. 'I can't wait to get back to civilisation, where people are normal and predictable.'

My brother had decided he was going back to London, seeing as Helen was obviously getting better. Soon there would be no thundering music shaking the walls of the house. The lounge would no longer be occupied by my brother playing his grand piano like some demented escapee from a musical lunatic asylum. As soon as Helen got up off her butt, the room would be free for normal use, i.e. for me to use it as a substitute putting green.

The neighbours hadn't stopped visiting the house. Even Baseball Cap turned up occasionally, munching Mum's cakes and calling her *Missus*. They actually seemed to be becoming friends. Sullivan turned up at all hours, never offering me a lift from school and always arriving at *The Haven* before me. Often his car would be parked outside when I trailed in, worn out from the bus journey. The house had turned from a bleak spot on the top of nowhere to a community centre.

So when I arrived in early on the Wednesday after my four tries/109 golf score weekend to find the house empty except for M, Mozart and Tiger, it was a relief. I remembered Mum was due to take Helen for her check-up; where Ian was, I didn't know. I grabbed a cake or two and sat watching M and Mozart chase each other around. Mozart had a toy I'd bought for the kittens, a little furry animal on the end of a fishing line. He and Tiger could jump higher than the kitchen cupboards to catch the thing, but M was always after it too. He wanted to drag the fur out of it. I was laughing at the way Mozart was leaping up out of M's reach when Mum's car drew up. *Clatter, clatter, clatter.* Helen came in on crutches.

'Cool! Give us a go.' I took them from her as she sank

down on a kitchen chair. She'd been in a right sulk since she'd learned that her insurance wasn't going to pay for a new car. She'd be lucky to end up with some clapped-out, second-hand wreck – not her style at all.

But now she smiled and let go of the crutches. 'It's hard work, I can tell you. My shoulders are aching.'

I was moving around the kitchen fast, getting a real swing as I sailed along. The pets scattered. 'Check-up okay?' I asked.

'Tell him, Mum,' said Helen. 'He won't believe it if I tell him.'

My heart skipped a beat. 'What? What is it, Helen. Are you okay? What's happened?' I sounded as panicked as I felt.

Helen looked at me in surprise. 'No, no, David, it's a good thing.' She put out her hand and stroked mine. She was grinning. I exhaled again. 'Then what is it?'

Mum was still taking off her coat and didn't answer for a moment. Time froze as I imagined what had brought that smug smile to Helen's face. She'd taken to littering the place with magazines that had bloodcurdling titles like *Brides' Bible* and *The Bride Beautiful*. If Sullivan had proposed, Mum would start using that fluty voice she uses on the phone: *Marvellous news ... yes, deeply in love ... planning a wonderful wedding.* I stopped swinging on the crutches, paralysed with horror as a truly awful thought occurred to me. *They would want me for a pageboy!* No way were they getting me into a frilly shirt and a kilt.

Mum took her time about answering and all the while

Helen just sat beaming, but finally Mum said, 'Helen's a genius.'

What could I say to that? 'When did they change the criteria for qualification?'

Helen gave me a dark look. She couldn't wait any longer to tell me. 'Actually, it's official. I have a genius IQ. They did some tests at the hospital because I had a fracture, here.' She pressed the front of her forehead where she'd hit the windscreen and I remembered the red stain like a bull's eye on the shattered glass. 'I scored 158 on the verbal reasoning tests. That puts me in the top category of Highly Superior. In other words, a genius. I am a genius.'

'Right, a genius who cleans other people's feet for a living,' I said. It was bad enough having McFeeble as some sort of musical whiz kid, I could do without a brilliant sister.

'I've told you before, I give pedicures sometimes. I'm not a chiropodist!'

'Well done. Excellent verbal reasoning there, Helen, but it won't wash.' I thrust the crutches at her.

'I'm a Mastermind,' she sang. 'My intellect is above superior. I'm a genius.' She babbled on. I left her to it and went into the lounge to putt. When I tired of that, I began sock golf so I could practice my driving and chipping in the house: a rolled-up sock enabled me to practice my strokes without damaging too much of the furniture. I'd just played a brilliant dogleg par four from the front door into the far end of the lounge when McFeeble came in and sat down at the piano.

'Get out. I need to practice,' he ordered.

I guessed he'd heard Helen's news and didn't like it any more than I did. He liked to think he was the only talented one in the family. But he wasn't going to take it out on me.

'I was here first.'

'The piano's in 'ere, moron. Wot am I meant to do – carry it out on me back?'

'Yeah, the piano I *bought* for you.' I ran my fingers over the keys. When great-uncle Albert died, I found his war medal and we had sold it for shedloads of money – most of which I gave to Ian because his first piano had been destroyed in the The Great Fire. And here he was, talking about *me* owing *him* a favour for carrying my golf clubs a few hundred yards!

'Leave it alone! No way is a primitive like you gonna play this. You'd have to lose your gills and grow opposing thumbs first.'

'You calling me primitive?' He was using the piano as a shield so I couldn't get near him.

'I'm gonna make a living out of music,' he said. 'I'm gonna make the Stirlings rich and famous.'

'Give me a break! Even classical musicians can't be mingers.' Though Ian had been a nauseatingly angelic-looking kid, with blonde hair and a cherub's face, he had deteriorated rapidly. 'Look at you,' I taunted him.' You've got the muscle mass of an eight-year-old girl. And stand up straight, you look like an old woman.' Ian in tight leather trousers on *Top of the Pops*? Nightmare.

'You owe me,' he reminded me, as I knew he would. I

took one last swipe of the sock and sent it slamming up against the window. Then, after telling Ian exactly where he could put his piano, I left him to it.

If it hadn't been for that conversation, I'd have returned to *The Haven* after school the next day. Instead, I decided to give golf a break while Ian was in 'precious musician' form and instead go with Abbas to his house after school – at least *his* Mum made a fuss of me and fed me and made me feel like I was welcome! But if I hadn't been in Dublin at that time, I'd never have seen what I saw. And that would have saved a whole lot of trouble.

Bad idea

Abbas' house was okay. He was lucky because he had *younger* brothers and sisters, so he was the first to do things, not the last. They listened to him as if he knew a thing or two. No one ever called him a moron. And his Mum was quiet. She hardly spoke any English. They'd moved from Sri Lanka and settled in Dublin, in the same street where we'd had two houses. And we'd stayed with them after The Great Fire, when we'd been sort of refugees ourselves.

Back in his house, Abbas demonstrated some techniques he'd learnt at karate. He'd joined a class in a community hall just ten minutes from Highfield Road. He hadn't got as far as earning any belts yet, but he was going to take his first test soon. He demonstrated the *yoi position*, which is where you stand, legs apart and fists clenched. On a shouted instruction you're meant to bend your front leg and lock your back leg. Don't smile. Then punch, swift and sure, at an imaginary opponent. The punch reaches the target in a straight line, like a bullet from a gun. It was wicked.

Abbas' Mum fed us after we were finished attacking imaginary opponents. His brothers and sisters were full of questions about where I lived – they hadn't been outside Dublin and I'm not sure they really believed my stories about cows and winding lanes and friendly nutters!

I left Abbas' house at about 8.30, in time to catch the last bus home. As I walked along, I was thinking about how things had changed over the last while. Before Helen's accident, I'd had a list of problems to be solved, but things weren't looking too bad now. Sure, Helen was still going out with my rugby coach, but now that I'm out of the A team, no one – not even Frazier – can accuse me of being a favourite. And I'm earning my way back in. Four tries in one game: that speaks for itself. I'd had no run-ins with Sullivan for a while. The night of Helen's accident, without words, we seemed to reach a sort of understanding, an understanding that we were on the same side, rooting for her recovery. He spent too much time at *The Haven* for my liking, but more and more I was remembering why he'd once been my hero.

And I'd begun to like country living, which was an unexpected bonus. The countryside is not all winding roads and crazy inhabitants with winding minds, though there are enough of those. There's Andrea, for a start. I knew her now and we were getting on. There's golf courses in the country, too. When I'd cut my handicap, Andrea would be impressed and I might finally get my chance to show her how to swing a club!

I was just approaching the bus stop, eating a Mars Bar and feeling very content with myself, when something stopped me in my tracks. There was a pub across the road from the bus stop, and out of it came Sullivan. He wasn't alone. He had his arm around a skinny brunette. She was tall and dressed in bright yellow, like a canary. She clung to his arm and they were laughing. She looked at him adoringly. They stopped and she put her hands on his cheeks and plonked a kiss on his forehead. He gave her a bear hug, kissed her, whispered something, then looked up in my direction. It was getting dark, so I couldn't be sure if he'd seen me, or if he just happened to look my way. I scrunched the Mars Bar wrapper into a ball and threw it down. When I looked up again, they were walking to his car. He ran round to open the car door for her, then they zoomed away.

There was a leaden weight in my stomach and it wasn't just the three Mars bars I'd eaten on top of dinner. I couldn't deny it: Sullivan was seeing another woman. Helen was at home, on crutches, with *Brides' Bible* and *Beautiful Bride*, while he was here, with another woman. Who was the genius? Not Helen, obviously.

The bus arrived and I climbed on. I sat by the window, down the back, and tried to figure out what I should do.

Should I tell Helen? She should know that Sullivan was treating her badly, shouldn't she? And she was my sister – I had to protect her from getting hurt. But then, all I could hear in my mind was Mum saying, *'Helen's had a terrible time lately.'* If I told her about this, would I just be making things worse? Maybe she needed Sullivan to help her get better. If she didn't have him, would she not care about getting well again? Then again, if I didn't tell her, I'd be storing up more trouble for her that would erupt later. Suppose Sullivan did propose? The whole wedding thing would start – dresses, flowers, Helen proud and happy – and he could still be seeing the canary-yellow woman. I could just see it now. We would get to that bit in the wedding ceremony when the guests are asked, *do you know of any reason why these two should not be bound in holy matrimony?* And I'd be the pageboy who grassed on the groom. Or was I meant to keep this secret forever?

My head hurt. I didn't want this. I didn't want the responsibility of telling her – there'd be tears, sulks and scenes and she'd be really upset. And I didn't want the responsibility of *not* telling her, of Sullivan getting away with it and treating her like a fool. What was I going to do?

By the time I got off the bus near *The Haven*, I still hadn't made up my mind. When I went into the house, I found Helen and Mum sitting on the sofa watching a film. Helen had her foot resting on a stool, with a salad on a tray in front of her.

I took a carrot off her plate. 'Okay?' She smacked my hand away.

I threw myself on the other sofa. Starting a conversation wasn't easy.

'What yer watching?'

'A film. *Love Has Its Reasons*.' Dreamy music was coming from the screen.

I groaned. It sounded like some romantic nonsense that would stuff her full of another *happily ever after* ending. If she'd been watching *Terminator 3*, I'd have had some hope she could handle her boyfriend.

'Sullivan not coming round tonight?'

'*Mr* Sullivan to you. And no, he's got some schoolwork to catch up on.'

Never heard it called that before. I grabbed another bit of carrot and jumped up the stairs to Ian's bedroom.

'Ian!' He was packing. I watched him for a while.

'Don't come in my room while I'm away,' he said.

'Don't worry, your poxy CD collection's safe with me,' I assured him.

'Ian … what would you do if …'

He was trying to pull the zip closed on a bulging suitcase. I did it for him, without mocking his lack of strength. He was the only person I could ask about this.

'If what?' he repeated.

'If … you saw someone with someone else they shouldn't be with?'

'Wot you on about, baby bruvver? Who?'

'Well, just for example, if you saw … say, Dad with another woman?'

'You've seen Dad with another woman?' he shrieked.

'No!'

Ian laughed. 'Because if you had, I'd say, kick away her white stick! Get it?'

'Yeah, I get it, but really, what would you do?'

He looked at me seriously. 'I don't know what it is you've seen, Davy, and I've a feeling you're not going to tell me.'

I looked down at my feet and didn't answer.

'Look, mate,' he said gently. 'Whatever it is, if you want to tell me, I won't tell anyone else. But if you don't, then my best advice is don't get involved. Other people's love lives …' He gave a whistle and shook his head. 'It's just very complicated. It's best to stay out of it and let them figure it out for themselves.'

It turns out I could be wrong about something

Next day Dad got off work early (it must have been a slow day for data) and gave me a lift home from school. It was a bright, sunny day, just when the country-side looks its best, so he started congratulating himself on our move. 'It's really worked out well, hasn't it? New hobbies, fresh air and friendly neighbours. Do you know, your mother and I have received three dinner invitations since Helen's party?'

'Great. I'm thrilled for you,' I said. I was delighted if they'd dismissed any thoughts of returning to the city, but I like to dampen parental enthusiasm of any kind. Having an enthusiastic parent is a bit like having a kid with Attention Deficit Disorder – tiring.

'Yes, we've moved into a good old-fashioned community,' Dad went on, gazing over the rolling hills.

'With good old-fashioned psychopaths.'

'What are you talking about?'

'Haven't you noticed some of them are, how shall I put this, a tad peculiar?'

'I don't know what you mean, Davy. These country

types are the salt of the earth.'

'Oh yeah? How about Baseball Cap? You know, what did Mike say his name was? Declan. Remember? Mike said he'd done something to his wife. Probably killed her and got her buried amongst all that wood and stuff.'

'You mean the old fella that ate his way through the buffet?' He thought for a while. 'Oh, that was on the day of … yes, I remember. No! Mike didn't say he'd done something *to* his wife. He said, "all he'd done *for* his wife".'

'You sure?'

'Now why would Mike say the old fella had done his wife in? I hope you haven't been spreading slanderous stories around the neighbourhood!'

We'd just entered the village. Dad had made me doubt my own senses. Perhaps Baseball Cap hadn't done his wife in. Perhaps Sullivan hadn't been seeing another woman.

'You know me,' I answered, 'tact is my middle name. Drop me here, will you? Thanks.' He stopped outside the village shop. I went in.

'Hi! How's the golf going?' The shop door clanged and Andrea was standing beside me in the '24/7'.

'Great. Haven't been out on the course since Old … since your granddad gave me a round, but I've been practicing lots. How about you? How's life in girls' golf?'

'Are you going to buy those?' asked the man who wasn't McDonnell, thrusting out his arm for the large brown envelopes I'd picked off the pathetic display of stationery. Was there a *No Talking* rule in this place? It was a shop, not a library – though granted I'd seen libraries that are more popular, and I'd known libraries that opened longer hours. I'd been the only customer until Andrea had come in, but anyone would have thought we'd slowed down a queue. I handed over the money.

'Let's get out of here.'

'How's Helen?' asked Andrea when we got outside.

I hesitated just too long before saying, 'She's getting better, thanks.' Females pick up on that sort of thing. If you're going to tell them less than the truth, you have to answer quickly and pick your words with care.

'What's wrong?' she asked immediately. 'Is it the head injury?' Male 0; Female 1. I started pulling the lever on the old village pump, trying to see whether any water would come out. Plus, I didn't want to keep talking to Andrea without staring – each time I saw her she looked prettier.

'No. She's going to be fine. It's not that.'

'What then?'

I looked at her: could I trust her? At least she could give me a female point of view, and it was driving me mad thinking about it. I decided to come clean. Male 0; Female 2.

'It's just, well, I saw her boyfriend kissing another woman.'

'The sod. What did she say when you told her?'

'I hadn't gotten around to the telling her part actually.' Andrea looked shocked. 'Do you think I should? She'll go crazy and get upset.'

'You've *got* to tell her. You can't let him get away with cheating on her like that.' She was talking the way Helen talked.

'You reckon?' The lever of the pump came off in my hand. Andrea laughed.

'I thought they were meant to make things better in the good old days,' I complained, propping the lever against the shopfront. I remembered what had happened to great-uncle Albert's glass ship: that had been antique and had crumbled like dust. I started telling Andrea about it as we walked out of the village towards Nutters Lane.

'My great-uncle had this ship made out of spun glass. It was red, white and blue with little figures of sailors climbing up the rigging. It's the first thing I remember about visiting him in England.' It was worth going to his crumbling old house just to see the ship and I'd made up stories to myself where I was a sailor on board it.

'What happened to it?' Andrea asked.

'It fell to pieces.' It had happened when I'd been helping Mum and Dad clear out Albert's house after he died.

'Fell to pieces in the same way the village pump did – all on its own?'

I laughed. 'No, it wasn't me, honest! I just took the protective case off and the whole thing disintegrated.'

'Shame.'

I wanted to tell her how I hated its destruction, that somehow I connected its loss with the way I felt about Albert's death, about things changing when you don't want them to, feelings that had come back with Helen's accident. Helen. But I didn't want her to think I was a wuss, so I changed the subject. When there's something important to be said, I just can't get it out. I prefer to make a joke, or sidetrack onto something else.

'Hey, how about a round of golf next weekend? Are you up for it?'

'Sure. Which day? Gramps might be able to take us on Sunday.'

That suited me fine. I didn't want to race back from rugby again; jumping out of a moving bus is no picnic!

'Sunday? Okay then.'

'I'll book a tee time and let you know, okay?'

'Sure. And, Andrea … about Helen and her boyfriend? Don't tell anyone.'

She smiled at me. 'Course not, David. But do think about what I said – your sister does deserve to know.' Male 0; Female 3.

I left her in Nutters Lane, heading into her granddad's house.

When I walked into school the next day I saw the familiar sight of the League trophy sitting proudly in the display cabinet outside the Headmaster's study. It was always polished and gleaming and I'd seen with my own eyes the Headmaster straighten his tie and smile at his reflection in the dazzling silver. We won it most years, so it had almost become a permanent fixture. Now he could kiss it goodbye thanks to the A team's pathetic performance. The season was lost. Some other school's name would be engraved on the trophy this time. Our record lately had been one disaster after another. The tries scored against us were so vast that, when added up, the total looked like a phone number. It was embarrassing, or it would have been if I were still on the team. Me, I was part of the solution, not part of the problem. No, let's face it – I *was* the solution. There was one last rugby prize we could win: the Schools Challenge Cup. Thanks to the fact that most of our fixtures for that fell early in the season, we were still in it. The semi-final was coming up soon. If I could get back in the team, I reckoned I could make a difference with my current form. We were up against Blackrock College, who always fielded a strong team, so it wouldn't be easy. But with Cahill in my position, the Headmaster would have to buy himself a mirror.

All week I trained, not just in after-school sessions but at lunchtime, too. I ran three laps of the sports field while everyone else was stuffing their faces. I went to the school gym to lift weights and did circuit training. During rugby practice I made every tackle as if it were the Cup final. McCaffrey, who was still standing in for Sullivan, gave me a pat on the back. I was determined to show that I deserved a place on the team, that I could win it for the school.

Friday came and report cards were handed out. What with my time off after Helen's accident and the fact that I'd been practicing golf every evening, I wasn't so confident about that. I was glad Dad had already bought me my Ping clubs as I reckoned I wouldn't be getting any rewards for my schoolwork this time round. The reports were always handed out on Friday afternoons. How considerate: making sure we had a whole weekend to have our parents bend our ears over any bad points.

I took mine onto the bus. As usual, it was inside a large brown envelope, sealed and marked: *To be opened by the addressee only*. The envelope was addressed to *Mr &Mrs Stirling*. All this made it difficult get a chance to have what Ian would call *a gander* before the parents pored over it like it was a map of Hidden Treasure. It was difficult to get a pre-emptive look, that is, if you were an idiot who didn't know how to buy a large brown envelope and print off a sticker addressed to your parents! I did, and had, so now I'd get to see just how bad my weekend was going to be.

I tore open the envelope and scanned the card. Certain words jumped out at me: *Satisfactory, Very satisfactory, Improving*. Sullivan had given me *Satisfactory* for History with no comment, so Mum and Dad would never have to know about the time I'd answered him back in class. Things looked good. Better still, certain trigger words weren't there. *Insolent* always got Mum and Dad going. *Must learn to apply himself* was another downer. There wasn't even our old favourite: *Must try harder*. Seems I do better at school when I take time off! Then I saw the comments for Games: *Excellent. David has regained his form after some poor performances*. *Excellent* was the top rating; St Joe's didn't go in for words like *brilliant* and *superb*. I kept looking at the Games entry, trying to work out what it meant for my rugby. Surely I would be back in the A team now? There'd been no change when the team lists were posted midweek: Cahill was still in the A team; I was in the B team. Changes were never made before a game, so I'd have to wait until Wednesday to see if I'd regained my place.

As the bus pulled into the village, I put the report card in the new envelope, sealed it and stuck on the address label I'd printed off. The weekend was suddenly looking very good indeed!

Back home, M was chasing Mozart and Tiger round the kitchen and the Genius On Crutches was kicking up a fuss. 'If those kittens trip me up, I'll kill them.'

'Hey, how do blonde brain cells die?' I asked, scooping up Mozart. I was trying to lighten the mood. *You've got to tell her.* Mum ignored me and Helen gave me a thunderous look.

'Alone!' I said and laughed.

I picked up a meringue. They were just the way I like them – crispy on the outside and gooey inside. *You've got to tell her.* I took another. 'Okay, if you don't like that one, how about this … What do you call a blonde with a brain?'

Helen scowled. 'Wash your hands! Those are feral cats you know. You don't know where they've been.' Tiger leapt towards Helen's left foot and she shrieked.

'Oh for the love of …' I grabbed a dog under one arm and a kitten under the other. 'What a fuss about nothing!' I was just heading upstairs when Mum stopped me. 'Not so fast. It's report week. Where is it?'

'Oh yeah, I nearly forgot.' I pointed Mozart at my school bag. 'It's in there.' Mum dived for it. I tried to put a look of concern on my face, but *Satisfactory*, *Very satisfactory* and *Improving* danced before my eyes. And *Excellent, regained his form* was the best.

McFeeble had gone to London. Pity. I could have done with a drum roll as Mum called me back.

'David, this is good.' She was trying to keep the surprise out of her voice.

'Naturally, Mother.'

'Let's have a look.' Helen held out her hand. I snatched the report card from Mum. 'No way! It's confidential.'

'I always got brilliant reports when I was at school, didn't I? Mum, tell him. I did.'

'What do you call a blonde with a brain?' I asked. 'A golden retriever!'

You've got to tell her ...

Not this weekend. I wanted a fantastic performance at rugby, followed by golf with Andrea on Sunday. Next week the lists of teams would go up and I should finish my lucky run with some good news there too. I knew I was being selfish, but looking at Helen, I just couldn't bring myself to say the words that would break her heart. I just couldn't.

A 'Star'

'**D**ad, fancy meeting me in the bar after my round of golf?' I was looking forward to a celebration. After scoring eight tries for the B team the day before – yes, eight, count them – I was charged up and all set for the game ahead.

'Don't mind if I do. Who are you playing?' Dad asked.

'Just Andrea and Frank Lynch.'

'That pretty red-headed girl? Well, take a word of advice, don't be too competitive. Women don't like it.'

I knew he was right. Helen used to cry when I thwacked a shuttlecock in her face. No matter how many times I explained *it was just a tactic* in badminton, she still threw a tizzy. I didn't plan to beat Andrea by much. I'd show her a few moves, make it more of a Master Class, then we'd walk off the course still friends – better friends than we were already. She wasn't like the opposition at rugby who had to be ground down, chewed up, beaten up psychologically and physically. I didn't want her crying or upset when I beat her, but I did have 'Gramps' to consider. Old though he was, he'd obviously been an ace golfer for decades. He'd beaten me 109 to 106 last time. I couldn't just coast around or he'd thrash me again. With all my practicing, I should be able to improve my score by three or four points for a win.

I arrived at the Starter's Office early. I'd been ready for hours. Andrea and Frank arrived, Frank pulling a buggy.

'Ready to play?' he asked.

'Sure.' I couldn't wait.

Then Frank said, 'I'm not going to play myself. I'll walk the course with you and Andy.'

My head swivelled round, looking for Andy Donaldson. This wasn't the plan. Yes, my long-term goal was to wipe the floor with him, but this was only my second round of golf on a proper course. I wasn't ready to meet him yet. My first thought was that Andrea had told Frank of my boast and he had arranged a competition between me and Dimbrook's best juvenile to save the club's honour. But where was he? There was no Andy in sight, just Andrea with a wide grin on her face.

'You can be a bit slow, can't you?'

Oh dear Lord! The sickening truth dawned: *she* was Andy Donaldson, Dimbrook's star. Andy Donaldson was Andrea.

'But … your name's *Lynch*,' I said. 'Andrea Lynch. Frank's your granddad.'

'Yes, but he's my Mum's dad. My name's not Lynch, it's Donaldson,' said Andrea. 'When she said the names, she made quotemarks in the air, like I had done when I'd talked of Andy Donaldson as the 'star' of the club. Male 0; Female 100,000,000!

There was nothing more to say. I'd said too much already.

I'd dug a big hole for myself. I looked like a complete idiot, so I kept quiet, kept my head down and rearranged the clubs in the bag as Frank Lynch said, 'We'll miss tee time if you two keep on talking. Are you ready?'

That was my cue to say *sorry*, *no* if I was going to. I could go home and stay hidden for a while. I'd behaved like a moron. I didn't have much to lose, but if I turned tail and ran, that would be another thing to be ashamed of. I'd stay. One good thing was that at least Frank didn't seem to know what I'd said to Andrea. She was laughing at me, but he wasn't in on the joke. And now I had no reason to hold back. I'd have to play the game of my life.

'Yeah, I'm ready,' I said, marching up to the first tee.

'Ladies first,' said Frank, like I needed reminding. Andy Donaldson placed the ball on the tee and took her driver out of her bag. Even the change of name made her intimidating and by the way she squared up to the ball, I could tell the place was like home to her. The crack as metal hit the ball was another giveaway and the three of us watched as it sailed straight and high.

'Nice one,' I muttered. *Don't be patronising* was what Helen said if I tried to cheer her up after some pathetic effort at physical fitness. Andrea just gave a little half-smile, as if she couldn't spare the time to talk.

I took my driver and placed a ball on the tee, feeling like an impostor. She was the golfer; all I'd done was hit a thousand or so golf balls at the range, in the grounds of *The Haven* and in the sitting room. I'd played more sock golf than real golf. I waited as long as I could before I swung at the ball. We didn't have to strain our necks to follow its progress: it hardly left the ground and landed about eighty yards up the fairway. Even Dad had done better than that! Frank Lynch said nothing, nor did Andrea. If this was going to be my standard, I'd end up with a score of 400+ and we'd finish the round on Tuesday of next week. I'd break records – all the wrong records.

But my rugby experience had taught me that nerves can ruin the finest player's game and that, once demoralised, you are your own worst enemy. I had to put my bad start behind me and focus on the game ahead. Most of all, the images of me boasting to Andrea about beating Andy Donaldson had to be forced from my mind. When Frank began giving me more local knowledge about the course, I made myself listen and concentrate.

For me, one poor shot followed another. 'Andy' had holed her putt before I'd got near the green. I stuck at it. She wasn't chatting, just letting her game do the talking. By the time we'd finished the fourth hole I was trying to calculate the likely difference between her final score and mine. She'd get around in just over par-75 or so, which is what professionals manage, while mine would look like a telephone number. I felt like snapping a golf club in two and marching off. Some days you are the pigeon; some days you are the statue.

It wasn't until the sixth hole, just after I'd teed off, that I heard the satisfying snap of club hitting ball correctly. I began to hope that I wouldn't be totally disgraced, just roundly humiliated. I made a six on that hole, and Andrea made a five. On the fourteenth, I made par and so did she. That was the high point for me – when I made the same score as her. After that I averaged double bogeys and ended up with a score of 103. I hadn't whipped Andy Donaldson's ass. She had a score of 73. She'd whipped mine.

We walked back towards the clubhouse. Andrea was still quiet, but she couldn't keep the buoyancy out of her step, the buoyancy I knew came from winning. I had to say something.

'Congratulations. You played well.' I tried to sound magnanimous, though my voice seemed flat; I couldn't hide the disappointment.

'Thanks, David.'

Frank Lynch had stopped to speak to some golfers he knew, so we went on into the clubhouse. Dad was there, leaning on the bar as if he was rooted to it. He raised his glass and started to say, 'Cheers!' when he read the look on my face and stopped. 'What happened? Who won?' he asked.

'Andy, here.' I indicated Andrea, knowing that, whatever the others were ordering, I was going to be eating humble pie.

'Andy?' Dad began his oh-so-convincing simpleton impression. 'You mean, *you're* the Andy Donaldson I've heard so much about?'

Andrea nodded. ''Fraid so.' She turned to me and asked, 'And you truly didn't realise it was me? That I was Andy Donaldson?'

'No.'

'Andy Donaldson, the juvenile Cup holder?'

'Why should I?'

'Well … because you kept seeing me with golf clubs, heading towards the golf club or the golf range. Because you knew Gramps was a keen golfer …'

'Okay, okay, I get it.'

'Admit it, you didn't think it could be me because I'm a girl?'

That was exactly it. 'If I apologise, can we forget it?' I said quickly. Frank had finished talking to the golfers and was heading towards the bar.

Andrea smiled a beautiful smile and put her hand on my arm. 'Oh David, I don't need an apology. I've got something much better. I've got a win!'

Dad laughed. 'Never forget Davy – the female of the species is deadlier than the male!'

Frank Lynch reached us. 'Well done both of you,' he said. Was he having a laugh, too?

'How'd you make that out?' I couldn't help asking.

'A score of 103 is not half bad. I told you before, lad, you're a natural.'

A *natural what?* Ian would have asked, but Andrea said, 'And 103 was better than my score on my second round,' which was generous of her, considering.

'I lost,' I reminded them.

'Now, there's your mistake,' said Frank. 'What was your score on that first round we had?'

'It was 109.'

'So, you've shaved off six points. Golf is essentially a

game where you are playing yourself. What is important is improving your own performance. You're doing that. Rapidly. Well done.'

As Dad bought us a round of drinks, I reflected on this. I wasn't sure I believed Frank, but it was something.

A few truths

Both Mum and Dad signed my report card – with flourishes – as if it were an international treaty or something. It was a wonder they didn't hand out commemorative pens. They were overdoing the parental encouragement, heaping praise on me, so I told them to calm down. No point raising their expectations too high. They used to freak if McFeeble got so much as one B grade. I find it's best to keep their hopes low, that way you avoid them getting disappointed and making your life miserable. They were only interested in the heavy subjects, so neither of them noticed the crucial entry – *Excellent. David has regained his form after some poor performances* – but I didn't point it out in case they sussed about my demotion.

'At last,' said Dad as we were driving into Dublin on Monday morning, 'I don't have to hang my head in shame when I go near St Joseph's.' He began talking about the glory days when Ian was at the school, winning prize after prize and they'd put on concerts in which he play the piano, play the violin *and* sing at the same time, like some one-man band.

I was staring at the report card. Something was bothering me. *Excellent. David has regained his form after some poor performances*. Suddenly it hit me: it was Sullivan's writing. McCaffrey was still running the squad, but Sullivan had written my report card. Why? I thought back to the scene I had witnessed on my way from Abbas' house. Sullivan kissing the woman in canary yellow on the evening Helen said he was catching up on schoolwork. I'd seen him clearly, but had he seen me? Was he trying to bribe me to keep my mouth shut? No, that was crazy. My Games performance was *Excellent*. I deserved to be back on the A team. So, why did it make me feel uneasy?

'Get a move on, Dad.' The traffic had slowed to a halt a few miles from school.

'What's got into you?'

'Don't want to miss Assembly ...'

On Mondays, the Headmaster read out the teams' results. I wanted to be there when he informed the whole school that, yet again, the A team had lost and the B team had won. But, more importantly, report cards were handed in before Assembly and I wanted to have a look at Abbas'. If McCaffrey's writing was on it, that would mean mine was the only card written by Sullivan, then I'd know for sure he was trying to bribe me to stay quiet. The traffic was still unmoving. I leapt out of the car. 'It'll be faster to run. See you, Dad!'

I ran through the streets, weaving my way through the suited men and women going to work. A few stragglers in school uniform were dragging themselves towards the school gates as the bell rang. I sprinted the last hundred yards, but the door to Assembly was closed. I'd missed my chance. Now I'd just have to wait until Wednesday when the team lists were posted.

I headed over for class. Surely the two most miserable words in the English language are 'school' and 'Monday', when you put them together it just gives you a shiver down your spine. But at least I had rugby practice to look forward to at the end of the day – that was pretty much all that was keeping me going at the moment.

After rugby, I was walking to the bus stop when a car pulled up beside me. It was Sullivan.

'Want a lift?'

I looked around. If anyone from my year saw me getting a lift from him, I'd be risking seeing the inside of a dustbin, face first. A bunch of sixth years stared, but this was like *The Godfather*: Sullivan's offer was one I couldn't refuse.

'Err, okay.' The plus side was that I'd be home at least an hour earlier than if I'd taken the bus.

We drove along. He didn't talk and I wasn't going to.

We'd got out of Dublin and were driving fast down a country lane, but Sullivan had just his right hand on the wheel. He sort of turned to me with what he probably thought was a friendly smile, but which looked uncannily like Hannibal Lecter after a good meal.

'How's the golf going? Helen said you played on Sunday.'

It got me the way he said *Helen*, as if using her first name stuck in his throat because he was talking to me. I was calling her *Helen* way before he came on the scene.

'I lost.'

'Well, you can hardly expect to win at this stage. Golf is like chess, you have to lose the first fifty games.'

'Thanks. I'll remember not to take up chess.'

'I didn't get a chance to play until I was at university. You're a lucky fella, Davy.' Hearing him call me *Davy* was like hearing Mum use a swear word. We drove along with just the noise of the windscreen wipers.

'Who were you playing?' he asked finally.

If I said *a girl*, a 'young lady' he'd met, he would laugh.

'Andy Donaldson, the juvenile champion.'

'Oh, okay then, no disgrace there.'

I reckoned he was actually trying to be friendly. I kept waiting for him to ask me whether I'd been anywhere near Hannigan's Bar last week, but he turned the subject to football and then we were home, me with an extra hour to my day.

I had a snack, took M for a walk and then took my clubs out into the garden to drive some balls. I was replaying every shot of the Sunday game. If I hadn't mishit the first ball, I reckoned I would have played a better round. That had thrown me, though I had made a partial recovery after the fifth hole. There were some cracking shots in amongst the 103. The advantage I had was strength. Andrea's shots were deadly accurate, but she couldn't hope to drive the ball two hundred yards. I could. If I could combine accuracy with power, I was made. I took my pitching wedge and started bombarding the garden shed with balls. Each one made a sharp cracking noise. Then I stood with my back to *The Haven*, driving the balls out, across the rough grass.

I had a hundred practice balls and I'd used nearly all of them when Mum called me in for tea. Sullivan's car was still in the driveway, but hunger was calling me in. The light was fading as I swung one last time. *Crack!* The depth of the noise told me I'd hit a powerful shot, but I'd hit it to the side, what they call a *shank*. The ball flew over the hedge into the lane beyond. I heard a weird sound, then silence.

I hesitated. Were my eyes playing tricks in the twilight? I thought I had seen a shape bobbing along above the line of the hedge and now it was no longer there. No, I must be seeing things. I gathered up my clubs and made for the back door, but turned back again. I dropped the clubs and ran towards a gap in the hedge. I peered through. Lying on the ground, his old bicycle beside him, was Baseball Cap. My blood went cold. I squeezed through the hedge, went up and shook him.

'Hey! Are you alright?'

No answer. He was lying in the middle of the lane. If a car came around the bend, he would be flattened in seconds. So, even though I'd heard you shouldn't move injured people in case they've got spinal injuries or something, I grabbed him under his arms and hauled him to the side of the road. I was hoping maybe he'd fallen off his bike because of a back problem, or poor eyesight, or a pothole, but there was a glowing red mark on the side of his head – right about the size of a golf ball. His baseball cap hadn't saved him. He slumped against the grass verge, still silent. My heart was beating madly. What if I had seriously injured him? Thoughts of Helen's brain surgery and how awful we all felt about it ran through my mind. This old fella didn't deserve that when all he was doing was cycling home.

I ran for the house. Mum, Helen and Sullivan were at the kitchen table. I was breathless. 'Mum, you know that old fella who calls you *Missus?* I think I've killed him!'

Mum let out a little yelp.

Sullivan leapt up. 'Show me!'

We raced towards the lane. At first all I could see was the bike. Baseball Cap had rolled into the ditch and was groaning. Was I glad to hear that groan! Then I saw it: the golf ball was lying in the ditch near him. I knew he'd seen it, and I knew Sullivan had seen it.

'Can you hear me?' asked Sullivan, pulling at the side of Baseball Cap's eyes. I'd seen him carry out the same proce- dure on rugby players. Thank God he was better at first aid than at dog handling.

Baseball Cap muttered something as Mum arrived on the scene. 'He's alive, thank goodness. Davy, don't frighten me like that.'

Me frighten *her?*

'We'd better take him to hospital, just to be sure,' said Sullivan. 'You stay with him while I get the car.' By the time he'd brought the car into the lane, Baseball Cap was able to climb in. The nearest hospital with an A&E department wasn't far away, so we sped off.

'What happened?' asked Baseball Cap. 'I was cycling along …'

Sullivan gave me a look, but neither of us answered. At the hospital I learnt Baseball Cap's full name. He was Declan Murphy, sixty-three years old, born in Ballykrieg and lived his whole life there – that is, the whole of his life he'd lived so far. I was still hoping I hadn't ended it prematurely. They sure want to know a lot of information before they treat you in hospital. Even I could diagnose his complaint: a large red bump on the side of his head that swelled by the second as I looked at it. But when he finally came out from behind the curtain, Baseball Cap was pleased.

'Just slight concussion. They told me to go home and take two Paracetemol.'

Two Paracetemol? *I* needed more than that after what I'd just been through. Concussing people brings on a headache, I can tell you. But was I relieved! As long as Baseball Cap wasn't going to sue me, I was in the clear. Though he'd been friendly enough since Helen's accident – what with his *Missus* and gifts of Guinness ads – there was a nasty side to him that I'd seen when I'd first found Nutters Lane. In the back of the car he was quiet, as if brooding on something. If he got at me about hitting him, I hoped Sullivan would be on my side.

After a silence of ten minutes, Baseball Cap spoke. He leaned forward until he was just inches from Sullivan's face.

'Here, youse like Brendan Sullivan.'

'I am Brendan Sullivan.'

'They said youse was courting the Stirling lass. We were debating in The Feathers – how long did youse play for Ireland?'

'Two seasons.'

'I was at Lansdowne when you scored the winning try against England!'

'You've got a good memory,' I chipped in, but Baseball Cap was off, giving a confused and inaccurate account of Sullivan's short, but illustrious international rugby career. We were back in Ballykreig, nearly home free at Nutters Lane before he returned to wondering just how he'd been knocked from his bike.

'I was pedalling along. Not a car in sight. There was a noise, like a whistle ... can you shed any light on it, boyo?' No, I most certainly could not!

We'd pulled up outside his cottage, just along from Frank Lynch's. Baseball Cap got out and Sullivan strode up to the front door.

'No earthly good you going there. That door hasn't been opened in years,' said Baseball Cap. He led us along the corridor formed by the bungalow wall on one side and the line of sheds on the other. He pushed open the back door and waved us in. We would've gone in – if there'd been room for us. The kitchen was full of junk, crates, boxes, more wooden *Guinness is Good for You* ads. The mantelpiece was crowded with photos of the same smiling woman – Baseball Cap's dead wife, I guessed. We stood in the doorway.

'My bike ...'

'We'll get that back to you,' I promised, ever helpful. You can't say I don't give good service when I knock some-one out. But it was Sullivan that Baseball Cap was focus-ing on.

'They'll not believe it when I tell them in The Feathers, that you've been in my home,' he said.

'Would you like an autograph?' Sullivan offered.

'You're the man.' Baseball Cap was clearly delighted and, after he had unearthed a pen lying under piles of papers, he handed it to Sullivan. 'On here,' he said. He thrust forward one of the Guinness ads.

'What shall I write?'

'To Declan. Best wishes ... very best wishes ...'

He could have *with love and kisses* if it were up to me, so long as he forgot what I'd done. We headed for the door, Sullivan striding ahead. I was just walking towards the door when Baseball Cap called me back.

'Here, boy, you forgot something.'

'Pardon me? I didn't bring anything in with me.'

'No, you left it behind in the lane.' From his pocket he took the golf ball. I couldn't say a word. I looked at it, then at him: how many kinds of trouble was I in? But Baseball Cap started to laugh. Had he lost it completely now? Was I about to be murdered where I stood?

'You look a bit shook, boy, are ye alright there? Here, I took up the ball so your mother wouldn't see it.' He handed it to me and I stared at it in my hand, still unable to speak. 'I know you think I'm long past it, but I was young meself and I got into a few scrapes in my time. It was just an accident, and we'll leave it at that. Anyway, I got an auto-graph out of it for the lads in The Feathers, so you did me a favour really.' He laughed again, and I backed away slowly.

'Thanks, I … it was really good of you not to tell.'

'Go on out of that and get yerselves home.'

I turned for the door again, to find Sullivan standing there smirking at me. 'Well, I've never seen you lost for words, Stirling. It was worth it for that alone.'

'Alright, alright, let's just go.'

We left Declan Murphy gazing at Sullivan's autograph. We went down the corridor of wood and corrugated iron. I looked through an open door to one of the sheds. Inside was a carpenter's workbench. Piled high in every corner were more old wooden ads. 'What are all these?' I asked.

Sullivan took one look. 'Imitation antiques,' he said.

'What! You mean he's a forger?'

'My God, Stirling, you really don't like to think well of people, do you? No, he's not a forger. Not quite. He's not breaking the law, just making loads of brand new bits and pieces look old.'

'Sort of the reverse of what Helen does for a living,' I said.

Sullivan laughed. 'They put all those "old" advertise-ments in pubs to make them look authentic. I was in one quite recently like that, with my mother. A place in Dublin called Hannigans.'

We were halfway down the front path when he said this and I stopped as abruptly as Baseball Cap when I'd hit him with the golf ball. 'Your mother?' I said. 'Your *mother?*' I thought of Canary Woman. Her hug. Their kiss. Just the sort of hugging and kissing I was always stressing to my Mum not to dish out in public.

Sullivan was looking at me as if I was concussed. 'Yes, David, my mother. What's the matter? Didn't you think teachers had mothers?'

'No ... it's just that ... your *mother?*' This was turning into a day of one shock after another: I needed to sit down.

'How many more times? Yes, when I was with *my mother.*' Obviously he hadn't seen me the other night and was baffled by my sudden, inexplicable interest in his relatives. I started walking towards the car again.

When we were back in the car, his tone changed. 'You got away with it this time,' he said, 'but be more careful in future when you hit a golf ball. You could have really injured that man.' I knew I should have walked home; I had almost escaped without a lecture. Mum would be at home, freaking out. She probably had me tried and convicted of Grievous Bodily Harm by now, in fact she was probably baking me a cake with a file in it to spring me out of jail. And he hadn't finished yet.

'I know you think I've been a bit hard on you lately. It hasn't been easy for you at school, has it, having your rugby coach dating your sister?'

'Too right.'

'If I've seemed hard on you sometimes, it's been because I've had to ensure that there's no question of favouritism.'

'Mission accomplished.'

'Precisely.' He went on, 'And try to think before you

act. Luckily, Declan doesn't seem to be too bothered how he was concussed. It was fortunate he was a fan of mine.'

'Yeah, what were the chances of that?'

Sullivan allowed himself another little laugh. 'You are one cheeky …'

And I laughed too.

Yummy!

'I've got some news.'

'*I've* got some news.'

'Mine's important.'

'*Mine's* important.'

Helen and I were in the kitchen, eyeballing each other, like we were about to fight a duel or something. A dead mouse lay by her feet, which Tiger had brought in and dropped by her as a 'gift'. She was sitting at the table, her crutches parked beside her. That's Helen, not the kitten. She was turning into a killing machine. That's Tiger, not my sister. Fortunately, Helen hadn't looked down so far. She'd been odd enough recently; she was bound to freak out at the sight of the harmless dead body beside her.

If I hadn't known better, I'd have thought Sullivan *had* been cheating on her and that, for the first time in her life, my sister was going to be the Dumpee, not the Dumper. But I'd done some checking and knew for sure that Canary Woman was his mother, like he said. I'd searched the Internet and found some pictures of him when he was on the Irish side, and there was Canary Woman in one of them, gazing at him as I'd seen her look outside the pub – adoringly. She was fit too, for a woman her age. Of course, that was another advantage of playing rugby: there were always some yummy-mummies about! I was relieved for Helen, and for myself. *You have to tell her.* Fortunately, I didn't. No scene where Helen went crazy and I had to give an account of what I'd seen as if I were a witness in a court of law. One less problem for me to deal with. And some good news to deliver, too – if I was ever allowed to spit it out.

'Great news. I'm playing in the A team for the Schools Challenge Cup semi-final.'

'Great, we're all thrilled for you,' said Helen dismissively. 'Now, I've got some *real* news. Life-changing, earth-shattering news.'

I'd have left there and then if I hadn't been hungry. I stayed, though I had a sinking feeling I knew what the news was – Helen engaged, loads of her beautician friends coming round, *oohing* and *aahing* about some ring, grief at school again as Sullivan and I came closer to being related. My nightmare of being a pageboy in a kilt was looming large once more.

'Okay,' I said, 'let's hear it.'

'Right,' said Helen. 'It's all arranged. I'm going to university.'

Mum looked as surprised as I was.

'With an IQ of 167 …'

'Hang on, Sis, it was one hundred and fifty-something last time we heard.'

'Whatever. It's still *amazingly* high,' said Helen, 'and I'm wasting it. I've applied and been accepted. I'll be at UCD by October.'

Mum clapped her hands together with delight. 'Wonderful! What have I always said?'

'So, you're not getting engaged?' I blurted out.

Helen laughed. 'What? At my age? With a genius IQ? I don't think so.'

From now on, she was going to be insufferable. I had said goodbye to the musical prodigy when McFeeble went back to London, now I had an at-home genius to contend with.

'Well, that is news,' I said. 'Oh, and by the way whiz kid, there's a dead rodent next to you.' She emitted a scream that travelled over the green fields …

I thought I'd see if I could find Andrea. She might be interested. At home, my news had been trumped by Helen's. I knew that when Dad came in, he too would want to hear every detail of her plans and news of my forthcoming game would disappear down the plughole.

I had waited for the team lists to go up that Wednesday with increasing anxiety. I told myself again and again that I'd earned my place on the A team, that with my Games report it was in the bag, but still a nagging voice inside me said it wouldn't happen. One thing was for sure: never again would I take my place on the team for granted. It had been hell being demoted, but at least the accusations of favouritism had stopped; Frazier hadn't uttered so much as a snide remark in weeks. Maybe, just maybe, it had been worth the pain. But I didn't really think so until the lists were posted and I saw my name on the A team. I was back! The semi-final was on Saturday. There would be one practice session with the team before we were fighting for our survival in the only competition we still had a chance of winning.

I took M for a walk. Funny, how I'd once thought Frank Lynch was a dognapper. People do things differently in the countryside, I suppose. They're odder, but friendlier. I guess M had wandered into Nutters Lane and Frank, realising he was no stray, had taken him in. That wouldn't happen in the city. Country neighbours, I had decided, were my kind of people!

I tried the driving range first and, sure enough, there was Andrea, a bucket of balls beside her, practicing her chipping. I told her about the game on Saturday. She paid more attention than I'd got at home, but since I had never owned up to being dropped from the side, I couldn't expect her to be pleased I was in the A team. She held M on the lead for a while, to let me have a go at chipping. She gave me a few tips about my grip and because I was still on a high, I let her.

Finally, when the bucket was empty and we were walking away, Andrea asked, 'Have you told her yet?'

'Her, who? Told what?'

She looked at me impatiently, 'Your sister. Helen. Have you told her that her boyfriend's a rat?'

'Err, no.'

She stopped. 'Why not? You really should, you know.'

'No, it's okay. He's okay. I spoke to him and–'

'Oh, right. What's this then, male solidarity? That is just *typical*. If you ...'

'No, no, Andrea, honestly, let me explain. The woman I saw him with was his mother.'

'*Mother*? And you *believed* him when he said that?'

'Yes, and I also checked the Internet, just to be sure, and there she was, with her son. It's definitely his mother.'

Andrea was laughing again. 'David! You said they were kissing *passionately*.'

'Well, I blame mothers. They shouldn't be so demonstrative in public. It confuses people.'

'Well, if you don't know the difference between a mother's kiss and a girlfriend's, you're in trouble ...'

I let M off the lead. We had to start running to keep up with him. The only way I could stop Andrea laughing was to out-run her. We began to race as we followed M over the hedge and through the fields. At least I could beat her in a sprinting contest!

Sullivan was back in charge at rugby practice the next day. He pushed us hard. If St Joe's didn't win the Challenge Cup, it would be the first year since he'd begun coaching the team that we hadn't won a trophy. That display cabinet outside the Headmaster's study would be half empty, the centrepiece gone. Saturday's game was crucial, and we all knew it.

The game

Friday evening, I ate two plates of pasta, which is great energy food, and took it easy, watching TV in my room. Tiger was lying on the bottom of my bed, feet in the air. Mozart nestled against my shoulder, so close that his purring filtered through the sound from the TV. I checked my mobile: McFeeble had texted, wishing me **'gd lck 4 ur gme'**, which I presumed was a good thing. I was feeling confident. All I needed was a good night's sleep and I was ready. Blackrock were going to be formidable foes. We needed to get ahead early in the game. For some reason I couldn't settle, something was niggling at me. I checked everything was ready – kit, boots, padding, socks, bag – all were there. It was too soon to start envisioning our winning moves. I'd do that on the bus on the way in to Dublin. Now, I tried to concentrate on the film, but couldn't. I went downstairs for a snack. The kitchen was empty. Helen was out with Sullivan – the first time without her crutches. Mum and Dad were in the living room watching something boring about birds on the Discovery Channel.

I found some cake and was eating it when Dad came in.

'Thought you were going to have an early night?'

'Can't sleep. Not tired.'

'I plan to do some gardening tomorrow. How about, when you come back from rugby, you set about building that rockery you promised?'

'Sure.' If I was still standing! Then I realised what it was that was bothering me. 'Where's M?' I hadn't seen him all evening. He wasn't in his basket in the utility room, or hiding in one of his favourite cubby-holes. I went into the garden to call him. No answer, but the gate was open. I went back in and grabbed his lead. He wouldn't always return to me if he was off tracking, but he would if he heard the rattle of his lead. Crazy mutt.

'Where are you going?' asked Dad.

'To find M.' I took a torch and my mobile. 'Call me if he turns up.'

I got away before Mum or Dad urged me to stay put. The last thing I heard was Mum saying, 'But I thought you had an important game in the morning?' Like I'd forgotten! But I wouldn't rest until I'd found M. I walked our favourite lanes, heading towards the centre of the village. One car nearly blinded me with full headlights as it came towards me, but apart from that the whole of Ballykrieg seemed to be asleep. Even The Feathers was in darkness, the car park deserted. The 24/7 was closed, too, naturally. I called out, 'M! Man of Honour.' My voice seemed to echo to infinity, but M did not appear.

My phone rang. It was Dad.

'Frank Lynch phoned. He saw M outside his bungalow.'

'Did he catch him?'

'No. By the time he'd got outside, M was gone.'

At least I had a sighting. I knew what direction to head in and I knew M was uninjured. I ran to Nutters Lane, with only the full moon and my torch to light my path. The lane was in darkness. I shook M's lead and called his name again. The light in *The Belfry*'s porch went on and a figure in pyjamas appeared in the doorway.

'That you David?' It was Frank.

I went to speak to him. From his account, half-an-hour or so had gone by since he'd looked out his front window and seen M rootling in the grass.

'Just like the first time. But I managed to get hold of him then. This time he was too quick for me.'

'Which way did he go?'

'Not along the road, or I'd have seen him.'

'You reckon he could still be in Nutters … I mean, in this lane?'

'Could be. I'll get my Tilly lamp.'

As I waited for Frank to put a raincoat over his pyjamas, I shone my torch across the gardens of the bungalows. It was eerie how different familiar places seem at night. Though most humans were sleeping, faint rustlings suggested that other life forms were awake and close by. The Earth is occupied in shifts by day-dwellers and nocturnal creatures and here I was, out and about in others' time.

Something led me towards Declan Murphy's sheds. If my crazy dog was tired by now and seeking safe shelter, the shantytown sheds offered just the sort of protection he would seek. Frank followed me as I made my way along the corridor that led to Declan's back door. The bungalow was in darkness and I was hoping its owner was soundly asleep: I didn't want Declan thinking we were burglars.

The first shed I entered was empty, but in the second a snarl came from beneath a load of *Guinness is Good for You* signs. I directed the torch and illuminated a dejected-looking M. He was like a drowned rat, his huge ears hanging down limply. His bid for freedom had ended as it always did – with him wishing he was home in the warmth of his basket. Relief flooded through me. Frank came round beside me and reached down, obviously under the impression that M would come quietly. He quickly withdrew his hand as M went for him. I pulled my jacket sleeves down, crouched by M and whispered gently, 'You are one crazy dog.'

He raised his head, then bared his teeth.

'M, it's me!' I began to say, knowing conversation distracted him. Then I pounced, grabbing him firmly by the middle. He tried to turn and bite me, but I'd learnt just where to hold him so he couldn't quite reach. I held him struggling in my arms. 'Thanks, Frank.'

'Glad to be of assistance. You'll be alright?'

'Yeah.'

I reckoned I'd walk by the side of the road to get home rather than go off across the fields. It would be all too easy to step into a rabbit hole and twist an ankle, and I needed all my speed tomorrow. As I attached M's lead and said goodnight to Frank, my thoughts returned to the make-or-break game. So much for an early night! So much for a relaxing evening! I was tired, very tired. The expression is dog tired. Now I knew why ...

I am running with the ball. The opposition is so close I can feel fingernails scratching my skin. I'm yards away from the touchline. There's cheering from the spectators. Andrea's here. She's cheering more loudly than anyone. She holds M on a lead. I throw myself forward. The ball meets the touchline. We've won! *We've won!*

I am running with the ball. The opposition is scratching at my arm. The touchline is ahead of me, but the faster I run, the more blurred and distant the line becomes. There's a strange noise. I don't know what it is. Andrea's here. She's yelling. She holds M's lead. M is missing. We've lost the game.

I woke up. Mozart was scratching my arm. I looked at the clock and hurled myself out of bed.

'I've missed the bus!' I yelled.

Down in the kitchen, Mum and Dad were in their dressing gowns, looking drowsy. M – the cause of my lateness – came up wagging his tail, full of energy and contentment.

'I'm late!' I yelled at them.

'You can take the later bus, can't you?' asked Mum.

'*No!* There is no later bus on a Saturday!' I shouted. 'Dad?' He was my only hope. If he drove me in right now, I might just make it.

'I was going to spend the day in the garden …' he grumbled, but he got up. I knew he was prepared to drive me in, but reluctantly. 'I'll just get dressed.'

'No time!' I yelled.

'He can't go in his dressing gown, David,' objected Mum. 'Supposing he's stopped. Supposing he's in an accident.'

'Then he'll be all ready for the hospital bed,' I shouted back as I leapt up the stairs to grab my kit. I wasn't going to waste time dressing either. I'd change in the car. I grabbed my bag and hurled myself down the stairs again.

'*Come on!*'

Dad's pace was infuriatingly slow. He drove slowly out of the driveway. Even the way he looked first right, then left, then right again before pulling out onto the road seemed more careful than usual.

'Let's get moving,' I shouted.

'Be quiet,' said Dad, with menace. 'I can't drive with you making all that noise. Anyhow, you'll be in no state to play if you go on like that.'

Yeah, so much for getting myself psychologically ready for the game. I pulled off my pyjamas and put on my rugby gear. The sight of my backside mooning out the window startled shoppers happily making their way into town.

Minutes ticked by. Though the roads were clearer than they were on weekdays, there was still enough traffic to slow us down. I urged Dad on, stressing the importance of the game ahead.

'It's our only chance. Do you get it? Our *only* chance. If we lose this …'

'Surely you'll be replaced if you don't turn up on time?'

That was meant to cheer me up!

'Of course I'll be replaced! And I'll be in deep trouble. *Just get me there!*' I was yelling again.

The game was being played on one of Blackrock's pitches, which had seemed a disadvantage up until now; it was along the M50 route, which meant we wouldn't have to drive through the city centre. Even so, the meeting time for the team came and went. By now they would all have realised I was missing. Sullivan would be asking, 'Where's Stirling?' He'd be talking to Cahill, ready to move him back into the A team. Damn! I had no phone. In the rush, I'd forgotten to bring it.

Ten minutes before the game started, we drove in through the arched gates of Blackrock College. I could hardly wait for Dad to stop the car before I leapt out and ran into the changing rooms. The team were all there, in their kit, ready.

'You're late!' shouted Frazier.

'Tell me something I don't know,' I yelled back.

Sullivan walked in. 'You're late.'

If I gave him the same answer, I was kissing goodbye to my place on the A team, and not just for one game but for the season. And I wanted to play. More than anything, I wanted to get on that pitch and score for St Joe's, so I bit back the words.

'Yeah, sorry,' I said.

'You know the rules,' he said. I didn't. I'd never been late for rugby before. Lessons, Assembly, detention, church – I'd been late for them often enough, but never for rugby. I waited.

'Have a one-page essay on my desk on Monday morning entitled *The Importance of Time*,' he said. 'Now get ready.'

I breathed a sigh of relief.

We marched out onto the pitch, surveying the opposition. They looked brutal and determined. The whistle went. Before we knew what had hit us, Blackrock scored a try and converted. Then a second, although they didn't make the conversion. We were 12 to 0 down and I hadn't handled the ball yet. Lack of sleep made me feel in a daze.

What the rest of the team's excuse was, I don't know. They were like zombies, wandering around vacantly while Blackrock took the ball and held it. We were being pasted.

Already I could imagine what it would be like after the game. The long lingering disappointment, the empty feeling that comes with losing. These were negative thoughts and Sullivan's advice returned to me. I conjured up pictures of winning: I race down the pitch, I score a try. It worked. I felt energy surging into me and the mental fogginess disappeared. Now I needed to get that ball and run with it. A fluke gave Frazier possession. He ran with the ball. I was free, ready for him to pass to me. I yelled to him, but he ran on, even though he'd seen me. He was ignoring the moves we'd gone through in training a hundred times. He was going for a glory run, but it was hopeless. He was tackled and Blackrock had the ball again. Then disaster! A penalty. A kick. 15 to 0.

I went up to Frazier and shoved him. 'Pass the ball next time, or ...'

'Or *what*?' He shoved back. Our team-mates came between us.

'Or we're going to bloody lose,' I shouted at him as the ball came into play again. I ploughed through, tackled and took possession, racing along the wing. I felt Blackrock players clawing at me, just like in the dream. My speed didn't desert me. I ran on, sidestepping a Blackrock player, then dummying another. I held onto the ball, hugging it to me, then threw myself down. The ball hit the line. A cheer went up from St Joe's: 15 to 5. Frazier converted to give us seven points. A long, mournful whistle drew the first half to a close. We dragged ourselves to the changing rooms, knowing we still had a mountain to climb.

Sullivan was there, looking concerned. 'Okay, I want 110% from each and every one of you. We can still win this thing. Nice try, Dave ... Stirling.'

The Blackrock team was slow to emerge for the second half. All they wanted now was the game to be over, with them looking forward to being in the final. We, on the other hand, had to make every second count.

'Get amongst it!' I urged as the ball went into play. Frazier tackled and took possession. As before, I paced him. I could see the shadow ahead of him. He was about to meet the huge, immovable object that was their fullback. Frazier swung round and passed the ball to me. I weaved towards the line. The fullback collided with me head-on. I rolled, still clutching the ball, picked myself up and ran on. Five yards from the line, I dived towards it. A try! 15 to 12. Frazier stepped forward for the conversion. I closed my eyes, pleading the ball to go over. It did! Now it was 15 to 14: we had a real chance.

We were making all the play. Blackrock had given their best and were now dragging their feet, hoping it was enough. With ten minutes it was still 15 to 14 and Blackrock were defending their territory like lions. I could see my team-mates were starting to tire, but we couldn't let go now. Again and again we ran at them, only to be knocked back. Time was running out.

'How long left, ref?' we shouted.

'Last play,' he answered.

We had one chance and one chance only to win. Black-rock were still time-wasting, throwing the ball to each other, but they did it carelessly and we took possession. From Frazier to me again. I had one final run to make. The mammoth shadow of the fullback was ahead of me and I didn't know if I had the stamina for another bone-crunching tackle. Suddenly a picture of how Johnny Wilkinson won the World Cup for England in 2003 flashed into my mind. It was a hell of a risk, but I was going to take it.

I dummied to the left, then ran to the right, losing the fullback for a crucial few seconds – just long enough to pause, look up and sight the posts. I drop-kicked the ball. Time slowed down as the ball sailed high. The crowd fell silent. The ball seemed to hover, then dropped right over the post. Blackrock, 15; St Joe's, 17. Three short whistles. The game was over. *We'd won!*

We let out a mighty cheer. Our supporters came forward. I felt my back being slapped.

'Well done.'

'You're a star.'

'First rate.'

'Drop-kicking us to victory is getting to be a habit, Stirling.'

There was even a fella in pyjamas and dressing gown; Dad had stayed to watch despite his clothes, or lack of them. I was so wrapped up in the game, I hadn't even noticed. But now he was waving madly at me, giving the thumbs-up and I felt like all my birthdays had come together.

The Importance of Time

'So, how about this rockery?'

Sunday morning, a day of rest, and Dad was determined to drag me out into the garden. I slid my head under the covers, knowing escape was only temporary. It was pay-back time for those Pings.

The grass was tall enough for Mozart and Tiger to hide in it. I'd have to mow that, too. But before I started, I reckoned I should practice my golf swing. My shoulder ached from the heavy tackles I'd made against Blackrock, but who cared? Winning is better than Deep Heat for soothing muscles.

I was lining up a difficult chip shot when a yellow convertible pulled into the driveway. The couple inside waved to me. Looking the way they did, they could only be Helen's friends. The woman was wearing high heels that dug into the gravel, so she tottered slowly towards the front door. I saw Helen come out and peer vacantly around. She has perfect eyesight, but has taken to wearing a pair of Dad's reading glasses, which make seeing difficult. She was experimenting with a new look, apparently, to suit her student life. Combat trousers, pulled-back hair – they'd throw her out of the Beauticians' Union if they could see her now. She'd started to carry books around, too. Rebel Without a Clue.

I put down my clubs, picked up a rock and carried it to where Dad had decided the rockery should be. Then another. And another. Boring. Throwing was more fun than carrying, so I began throwing them. With the smaller ones, I could bowl them over arm, like a cricketer. I'd just hurled a rock towards the pile when Declan Murphy came up the driveway.

'Well thank God you missed me that time, boyo.' He gave me a wink and a culchie nod as he made his way towards our back door.

Five minutes later, Sullivan arrived. I kept on throwing rocks into a pile and just waved in his direction. He waved back, his walk buoyant, a winner's walk. I knew he was pleased with our win – not that it meant he'd forget the essay he'd given me to write, nor that the Final was still to come. Sullivan wouldn't rest until the Challenge Cup was sitting in the display cabinet and the Headmaster was smiling at his reflection in the silver. Neither would I.

The rocks were piling up. I had to search further afield to find them, and it was mind-numbingly dull.

'Walk!' I said to M. He bounded up. Andrea wasn't at the range, or at Dimbrook, but I found her outside the shop. She was reading the notice that the man who wasn't McDonnell had put up in the window:

BUSINESS HOURS

Open most days about 9am or 10am.

Occasionally as early as 7am, but Tuesdays as late as noon or 1pm because I visit my sister.

We close at about 5.30pm or 6pm. Occasionally about 4pm or 5pm, but sometimes as late as 11pm or 12pm.

Some afternoons, I'm not here at all.

Usually open Sundays, unless the weather is particularly good.

I laughed. 'But he still has 24/7 up over the door.'

Andrea was about to answer when a car screeched to a halt beside us. Someone was in a hurry! It was a large BMW, with a Dublin reg., and its owner looked like his blood pressure was boiling over. He pushed past us and grabbed the door handle, giving it a good shake.

'Don't tell me it's closed! I need a road map. Pronto.'

'Sorry, he's not open at the moment,' said Andrea.

The guy looked at her impatiently. 'Well, when will he be open?'

Andrea and I looked at each other.

'Probably not at all today, given the weather,' I said.

The man looked at me like I was insane. '*Weather?* What the hell's that got to do with the price of bread?'

'Angling,' I replied.

'What …' he spluttered. 'What are you *talking* about?'

I was enjoying myself now. 'Angling, that's what he's doing, because the weather's nice. He's down at the river for the day, of course.'

He looked at me like I was part of some dangerous conspiracy. 'My God, why I venture beyond Dublin, I do not know. You people are … *nutters!*'

He jumped into his car and sped away, and Andrea and I laughed until our sides ached. Finally, Andrea looked up and said, 'Playing golf today?'

'Might go to the range later. I'm in the middle of building a rockery.'

'*Wow!* How do you do that?'

'Difficult. It requires meticulous planning.'

'I'm walking back that way. I'll take a look.'

'Of course it doesn't look anything much yet. Did I tell you we won our rugby game yesterday? We came back from twelve points to five. I scored from a drop-kick in the final minute.'

I gave her a detailed description of every minute of the game. She looked interested. As we climbed the hill to *The Haven*, she saw Sullivan's car parked in the driveway.

'So that's the boyfriend who kisses his mother in public,' she teased.

'Okay, okay.'

'And you really couldn't tell the difference?'

'It was dark.'

'Oh right! Perhaps I'll have to show you the difference.'

That was definitely an offer I wouldn't refuse. She raced to the house and I invited her in for coffee. The kitchen was crowded. Helen was talking, but no one was listening to her – just staring. Her blonde hair was gone. She'd dyed it the colour of a London bus.

I gave a mock scream and noticed that Sullivan gave me a look of agreement before converting it to an appreciative smile.

'What have you done, you freak?' I shouted. 'Where is my sister? What have you done with her?'

'Give it a rest,' said Helen. Her fingernails and lips matched her hair.

'I *love* the look! It's *so* you,' said the woman in impractical heels.

'I guess this is what they mean by beauty comes from within,' I said. 'It comes from within jars, within bottles …' but I shut up when I saw Andrea was looking at Helen with admiration.

'Hey,' I said to Declan Murphy, 'how far do you reckon you can throw a rock?'

He took up the challenge, and Sullivan did too. Even the fella who'd come with the woman in heels had a go, though his throw was as weak as a baby's. Andrea beat him by miles.

It was dark when they all left, so, as per usual, I would have to finish my homework in the car on the way to school, but I decided to get that essay out of the way before bed.

The Importance of Time

Time is important. Time stops everything happening at once. If there was no time, the school timetable would be a joke. Everyone would turn up at the same classroom together. There'd be crowds, loads of pushing and shoving. It would be very confusing.

Or, more likely, nobody would turn up at all. There'd be no such thing as being 'unpunctual', just a bunch of teachers going crazy, staring at the wall where the clock should be, asking, 'Where is everybody?'

Then I was stuck. I found Helen in the kitchen, alone.

'Okay, Einstein, tell me something to write about time.'

'Einstein's General Theory of Relativity,' she said, whipping off Dad's glasses so she could actually see me, 'conjectures that space and time, or space-time …'

'Slower!' I was writing it down.

'Einstein's theory states that space-time is curved by gravity.'

'Thanks.' I went back to my bedroom with a few more lines to add.

According to my sister, who's been certified a genius by some quack doctor, Einstein's General Theory of Relativity states that time and space, or space-time, are curved by gravity. Curved, so that must mean we'll end up meeting ourselves back where we began. Things should happen over and over again like in 'Groun-dhog Day'. I wouldn't mind Saturday happening all over again, because I played rugby and my team won, but there are other days that are bad enough happening the once.

The expression 24/7 means all time because there are 24 hours in a day, 7 days in a week. There are no gaps in 24/7. It's watertight.

Mozart bounced onto my bed, pursued by M. The kitten's ears were pink and wet because M had licked them so much. 'Okay, you two, time for bed,' I ordered.

Someone who doesn't know the importance of time is my dog, who went missing the other night. It could have been Christmas Day for all he cared. So I had to find him even though it was past midnight and I had an important game the next morning. Which <u>we won.</u> So, it's not me but my dog who needs to know the importance of time, and since he doesn't wear a wristwatch, it's never going to happen.
David Stirling.
(Time: 10.56pm precisely)
 P.S. After a bit of time's gone by, you realise some people aren't as bad as you thought they were.

David! If you're not ready and down here in five minutes, I'm leaving without you! David? *David!*' There was a crash and a yell, followed by the sort of language that gets me a detention at school. Dad had tripped over M – again.

Ready? Was I *ready* for school? I lay in bed thinking about this as curses and growls floated up the stairway. Overall, yes I was. I was ready for Assembly where the Headmaster would read out the rugby results, ready for the pats on the back I'd receive from my friends. And I was ready with my essay for Sullivan. I was ready for whatever the day had to throw at me.